CHARLES DICKENS' OLIVER TWIST IN EASY READING VERSE

By the same author:

Shakespeare's Tragedies in Easy Reading Verse

Shakespeare's Comedies in Easy Reading Verse

Shakespeare's Histories & Romances in Easy Reading Verse

Shakespeare's Sonnets in Easy Reading Verse

Chaucer's Canterbury Tales in Easy Reading Verse

Charles Dickens' A Christmas Carol in Easy Reading Verse

Kenneth Grahame's The Wind in the Willows in Easy Reading Verse

CHARLES DICKENS'
OLIVER TWIST
in Easy Reading Verse

Richard Cuddington

Contents

OLIVER'S BIRTH IN THE WORKHOUSE

In a place called Mudfog,
A dark, dank English town,
On a winter's afternoon,
Just as the sun went down,

Within a public building,
All grim and grimy grey,
Caught by the last receding light
Of a dismal day,

A little child was born – and in
The Parish Workhouse there.
The mother who gave birth to him –
A frail young girl, but fair…

Lay gasping following the birth,
And very close to death,
While her new feisty baby boy
Fought hard for his first breath.

Eventually the little child
Sneezed and breathed and thus,
He entered this uncertain world
With minimum of fuss.

He looked out for himself and this
Was really just as well,
Because the only help he had –
We sadly here must tell…

Was from the Parish surgeon
Who worked just for his purse,
And with him was a drunken hag
Who acted as a nurse.

When the little baby boy
Let out his first loud cry,
His mother whispered in strained voice,
'Oh please, before I die,

'Let me see my darling child.'
Her poor sad face was set.
The surgeon with some kindness sighed,
'Don't talk of dying yet.'

'Lor bless her heart!' the nurse exclaimed ,
'What a way to speak.'
She hid a bottle as she spoke
And how her breath did reek.

'When she has lived as long as me,'
The nurse all slurring said,
'Had thirteen children of her own,
And all but two are dead,

'And those two in the workhouse now —
Well, 'twould be true to say,
She would know better than to then
Be carrying on this way.'

The mother stretched her hand towards
Her crying little child;
Her face was tear stained and her eyes
Looked loving and yet wild.

The surgeon placed the baby in
The crook of her small arm,
And for a moment in its life
The child was safe from harm.

Held by his loving mother,
All snug and warm and curled,
In quite the safest place of all
In this old troubled world.

With cold white lips she kissed him.
The little baby cried,
Then with wild eyes she gazed about,
Shuddered — and then died.

'It's over Mrs Thingummy,'
The surgeon said at last.
He spoke with resignation;
He didn't seem downcast.

'Ah, so it is – poor dear,' the nurse
Looked down and then just shrugged,
And then she saw her bottle cork
Had somehow come unplugged.

It lay there on the pillow,
Just by the dead girl's head.
She grabbed it – then the surgeon spoke,
'Best see the child is fed.

'Give it a spoon of gruel – that's all.'
He took his hat and cane.
He sighed, 'I think we can expect
Another bout of rain.'

He paused then by the bedside
And looked down at the girl.
Her worn and fragile face was like
A white and precious pearl.

'She was a lovely looking lass.
Wherever was she found?'
The nurse replied, 'Out in the street.
Just lying on the ground.

'Her shoes were worn to pieces.
She looked a frightful mess.
Where she had come from – heaven knows.
It's anybody's guess.'

The surgeon took the girl's left hand,
Delicate and white.
'The usual tale – no wedding ring!'
And then he said 'Goodnight.'

He left the room intent now on
His dinner – out somewhere.
The nurse then took a mighty swig
And sank into her chair.

The little baby boy was wrapped
Within a blanket which
Was overdue in needing
A skilful, timely stitch.

So there the baby lay and cried,
A Workhouse orphan who
Would be a Parish child, half starved –
Unloved – uncared for too.

And he'd be cuffed and buffeted,
For this was always done,
Despised by all and made a drudge,
And pitied by no-one.

So he cried out – and lustily –
And if he'd known the score,
I think it's safe to say that he'd
Have likely cried much more.

MR BUMBLE VISITS MRS MANN

The first thing that the Parish did
Was give the child a name;
They didn't give much thought to it,
'Twas always just the same.

As long as it was not yet on
The lengthy Parish list,
Then it would do – so he was called,
First Oliver, then Twist.

'Oliver Twist, yes, that'll do'
The overseer agreed.
The warden of the church concurred,
And so this simple deed…

Was all tied up and finalised,
The child now had its name,
And this would follow him through life
Whatever he became.

So Oliver was farmed out to
A Parish house close by.
A place for those of tender years
Where they would toil and cry.

And he was taken there within
A few hours of his birth;
A place where he received no love,
Accorded little worth.

The system took a special pride
In making doubly sure
That orphan's had scant clothing,
Sufficient – nothing more.

And it, of course, would have been wrong
To overfeed the lad,
For gluttony was such a sin –
Considered really bad.

So Oliver grew very used,
From just a few months old,
To being hungry all the time
And shivering from cold.

And so to sum it up we'd say,
Poor Oliver's young life,
Overflowed with huge neglect,
Indifference and strife.

~ ~ ~

'Twas Oliver's eighth birthday
And still he was within
The little children's Parish house –
Cold, hungry, pale and thin.

Mrs Mann, who ran the place
In an appalling way,
Saw an apparition
Outside the house one day.

It was the beadle she espied,
And Bumble was his name,
And he was at her garden gate
And having quite a game…

At trying to undo it –
The gate just wouldn't budge,
And Bumble there was kicking it
And getting in a fudge.

Mrs Mann went running out.
'My heart alive,' she cried.
'It's lovely seeing you today,'
But Bumble – fat and wide…

Just shook the wooden gate with force
And kicked it hard again,
Ignored her salutation
And made it very plain…

That gates obeyed fine beadles.
Mrs Mann just sighed.
'I'm sorry Mr Bumble,
I locked it from inside.'

She curtsied as she spoke to him.
He said in quite a state,
'You shouldn't keep a beadle
A-waiting at your gate.

'It's disrespectful ma'am – I'm here
On parish business thus,
You should be ready to receive,
With minimum of fuss.

'For I'm a Parish beadle…'
Oh, what a noise he made.
His self important attitude
Was clearly now displayed.

Finally he calmed right down,
And said, 'Well, Mrs Mann,
Lead the way – for I must now
Inform you of a plan.'

She ushered him inside the house,
Into her parlour where,
She indicated he should sit
In her most comfy chair.

And once he was well settled,
His hot air now expended,
Mrs Mann, with sweetness said,
'Now please don't be offended…

'For I would like to say a word
Before we have our talk,
And taking into full account
You've had a tiring walk…

'I wondered if you'd feel inclined –
For you have walked non-stop,
Well, would you like to – you know, sir,
Why, have a little drop?'

The beadle feigned a look that said
He'd never have a drink.
Not while on Parish business.
Whatever would folk think?

'No, not a drop,' he cried outraged.
But though he did resist,
She said, 'I really think you will,
And sir, I do insist.'

Mr Bumble coughed and said,
'It's but a little sin.
What is it ma'am?' and she replied,
'Why it's a spot of gin.

'I keep it for the children,
For it is good to quell
The sickness in their stomachs
When they're not feeling well.'

So Bumble had a little drop,
And bending his right arm
Another – then he, slurring said,
'And now to business ma'am.

'I'm sure you've been a-wondering
What I've come here to say.
Well, Master Twist – the orphan boy
Is eight years old today.

'I named the lad myself, I did.'
'You did?' the lady said.
'Oh yes,' the beadle answered.
'It came from in my head.

'I do it alphabetically,
The last one was an S,
So Twist I named him, to ensure
It's tidy – not a mess.

'Anyway, the reason that
I'm visiting today,
Is because the time has come
To take the lad away.

'The Board have just determined,
He's now too old I fear,
To carry on a-boarding ma'am
In your fine set-up here.

'They want him now to take his place
In the Workhouse where
He'll be looked after and will be
Safe in parochial care.'

Mrs Mann was quick to say,
'I'll fetch the boy right now.'
She soon returned with Oliver
And said, 'Now make a bow.

'Yes, to the gentleman you see
Before you – over there.'
The boy's deep bow was split between
The beadle in the chair…

And the cocked hat on the table:
He then heard Bumble say
In his loud, booming, measured voice,
In his majestic way…

'Now will you come along with me?'
Oliver replied,
'Can Mrs Mann come with me too?'
The lady puffed and sighed.

She embraced poor Oliver
As if she loved him so,
And made out with impassioned cries
She wished he wouldn't go.

'She cannot come,' the beadle boomed,
'But I confirm that when
You're settled in and feel at home,
She'll visit now and then.'

All of this was subterfuge.
The lady didn't care
If Oliver remained with her
Or if he wasn't there.

And Oliver, for his small part
Thought it would be most wise
To make it seem he liked her, thus
His earnest, fervent sighs.

They were a ruse because he felt
That all this was expected.
It wouldn't serve him if he showed
How he had been neglected.

And so the beadle, Bumble,
Took Oliver by the hand,
And suddenly young Oliver
Began to understand.

He thought that he was going
Far off and so his eyes
Were filled with giant, sobbing tears –
He filled the room with cries;

For he was leaving there behind
The only friends he'd known,
And he was now convinced he'd be
Put somewhere on his own.

OLIVER ASKS FOR MORE!

The beadle took the frightened boy
To the Workhouse where
He was to dwell – and where he'd find
Indifferent kind of care.

'You're an orphan,' he was told.
'What's that?' the boy had asked.
'The boy's a fool,' somebody said,
'But he should still be tasked…

'With gaining education,
So start him right away,
On oakum picking – let there be
No moment of delay.'

So Oliver, on that first night
Could be heard to weep,
But no kind hand consoled him as
He cried himself to sleep.

And o'er the coming months he found
That Workhouse life was tough,
And when it came to sustenance,
There never was enough.

For all they had at mealtimes
Was just a bowl of gruel,
And quite the smallest piece of bread –
So not sufficient fuel…

For growing children – what a way
To treat young folk in care.
It was inhuman, very cruel,
Wicked and unfair.

Such an awful system,
Uncaring, cold and mean,
About as sinister and dire
As any ever seen.

So all the little children
In the Workhouse there
Were wild with hunger, going mad,
And one boy did declare…

That if he didn't find a way
To get some more to eat,
He knew how he could get a hunk
Of tasty, wholesome meat.

He said he'd eat the weakly youth
In the adjoining bed.
The children all believed in each
And every word he said.

The reason was quite simple,
He had a hungry eye –
Wild and full of certainty
That told he wouldn't lie.

And so they held a council
To get this sorted out.
Their aim was simply, get more food.
They couldn't live on nowt.

And so they all agreed a scheme,
Who drew the shortest straw,
Would after supper had been served –
Then go and ask for more.

And who should draw the shortest straw?
Well, wouldn't you just guess.
It was poor Oliver, who now
Felt under massive stress.

But he had lost and so must act,
Thus on that very night,
Once the meagre gruel and bread
Had disappeared from sight…

Every boy's eyes fell upon –
And then began to stare,
At frail young Oliver, who sat
In desperation there.

He raised himself and driven by
Such wretched misery,
And hunger of a kind that most
Will never ever see…

Got up from where he sat – advanced
With bowl and spoon in hand –
Amazed at his temerity
But set to make a stand.

So he addressed the master
Who bestrode the floor
With callousness and awfulness –
'Please sir. I want some more.'

The master was quite overweight.
Quite obviously well fed.
A hearty man who always had
Three times his daily bread.

But he turned pale – oh yes he did.
He gazed quite stupefied
At this young rebel standing there,
Frightened and wide-eyed.

The master grabbed the copper
To give himself support.
He was astonished – mortified –
Quite overcome and fraught.

His helpers too were paralysed,
Their faces so severe,
And as for little Oliver,
He trembled there in fear.

Finally the master spoke,
And no, he didn't roar,
But softly said a single 'What?'
'Please sir. I want some more.'

The master aimed a savage blow
At Oliver's small head.
Then pinned his arms and shrieked aloud,
And now his face turned red.

When Bumble heard what had occurred,
Well, how that beadle roared.
He rushed off in a moment to
Address the sitting Board.

By chance they were then meeting,
When Bumble – in a stir –
Addressed the chairman and he said,
'I beg your pardon sir.

'Oliver Twist has asked for more.'
There was a general start,
And every member of the Board
Felt their own pounding heart.

And horror was depicted
On every florid face.
'He asked for more,' the beadle cried.
'Oh what a dire disgrace.'

'For more?' the chairman bellowed out.
'Am I to understand,
He asked for more when he'd been fed
By our own kindly hand?'

'He did,' Bumble replied and hit
The table with a bang.
Another man piped up and said,
'I know that boy will hang.'

And so the members of the Board
And beadle thus combined
To have poor, hungry Oliver
Taken and confined…

In a room all on his own,
And then no time was wasted
In getting rid of Oliver,
For a sign was pasted…

Offering five pounds reward
To anyone who'd take
Oliver from parish hands
And do their best to make…

A 'prentice out of him – and then
Do their best to raise
A better kind of person and
Force him to change his ways.

MR BUMBLE FINDS OLIVER A JOB

And now for one long bitter week
Oliver was entombed
Within a dreary cell and while
The beadle foamed and fumed.

And then a chimney-sweep came by
And saw the dismal sign,
He rasped, 'I need a 'prentice so
I'll make this young 'un mine.'

He went inside and saw the Board
And Mr Bumble too,
And they agreed a price each thought
Would be enough and do.

Not quite the five pounds on the gate,
But just enough to get
Poor Oliver as 'prentice –
And thus the deal was set.

So Oliver would be a sweep:
Climb chimneys with a brush.
A dirty, dangerous, awful job,
Removing filth and mush,

While getting grimy black with soot
And sometimes getting stuck,
And struggling there to free himself
Within the dirt and muck.

But now the deal was done and so
This seemed the young boy's fate.
Poor Oliver knew straight away
'Twould be a job he'd hate.

'Don't rub your eyes all red and sore,'
Said Bumble now with glee.
'You're going to be a 'prentice lad
And it's all thanks to me.'

'A 'prentice sir?' wailed Oliver.
His voice beset with strife.
The beadle cried, 'The Board my lad
Has set you up for life.'

But when scared Oliver was shown
The dreadful looking sweep,
He saw he had good reason now
To remonstrate and weep.

A dirty, scruffy, evil man
With no humanity,
And this was clear for anyone –
And Oliver – to see.

But there was nothing to be done.
His fate was set and sealed,
But still he cried and piteously
And inwardly he reeled.

So Bumble took the frightened boy
To see a magistrate,
To get it properly ratified
And seal the poor lad's fate.

The magistrate said, 'I suppose
He likes this chimney sweeping.'
Whilst seemingly quite unaware
That Oliver was weeping.

'He dotes on it your worship,'
Came Bumble's swift reply.
'If he can't be a chimney sweep,
The boy would rather die.'

But then the magistrate espied
The crying, trembling sight
Of Oliver, who he now saw
Was suffering from fright.

'My boy,' he said, 'you look alarmed.
Whatever is the cause?'
Oliver fell onto his knees
And, following a pause…

He cried, 'I beg you beat me
Or kill me, rather than,
Send me to be a chimney sweep
And with this dreadful man.'

'Well I never,' Bumble cried.
He raised his hands and eyes.
'What an artful orphan boy –
A one for telling lies.'

'Hold your tongue,' the magistrate
Spoke out and angrily.
'I beg your pardon,' Bumble cried.
'Did you just speak to me?'

'Yes, hold your tongue and do it now.'
Bumble was wide-eyed.
A beadle told to hold his tongue!
Well, he was mortified.

The magistrate now spoke some more.
'These indentures are rejected.
Take the boy back with you and
Make sure he's not neglected.'

And so once more the sign went up,
Five pound notes would be paid
For anyone now offering
A likely lad a trade.

Some time passed by and still there was
No opportunity
Presented to the Board and so
They thought, 'Why there's the sea.

'We'll send the boy aboard a ship
To work and cry "Ahoy".
Yes surely some good Captain must
Require a cabin boy.'

So Mr Bumble was dispatched
To check this option out,
And on returning, by the gate
And looking all about…

He saw the undertaker.
Sowerberry by name,
Who said, 'I've measured up the two
Who died – the very same.'

'You'll make your fortune outa us,'
The beadle said, then sighed.
'Just think of all the cash you've made
From all the waifs who've died.'

The undertaker sniffed and said
With sombre, down-turned face,
'The Board don't pay that much and so
It's really not the case.'

Bumble sniffed himself as well
And said, 'Now by the by,
Do you know anyone who'd give
A little lad a try?

'We're looking now to place a boy
For honestly – by 'eck,
This little lad has come to be
A millstone round our neck.'

The undertaker was all ears.
'Don't leave him on the shelf.
I'm looking for a 'prentice so
I'll take the boy myself.

'As long as we can both agree
A sum I can afford.'
Bumble nodded and then dragged
The man to see the Board.

Everything was soon agreed
And Oliver was told
They'd found an opportunity –
As rare as finest gold –

Working for a funeral man,
And if he e'er came back,
Complained or didn't try enough,
Was found sometimes to slack…

Well then the Board would have no choice
But send him off to sea,
Where he'd be drowned or knocked about –
That's just how things would be.

The Board had told the beadle,
'Remove him from our sight,
And take the rascal off at once –
Yes take him there tonight.'

So Oliver packed up his things
And pulled his cap well down
And went with Mr Bumble who
Walked on with rigid frown,

But with his head held high – the way
A famous beadle should –
And Oliver just followed him
The very best he could.

THE FUNERAL PARLOUR

Their destination was in sight
When Bumble's eyes cast down
To check on Oliver – and then –
His face took on a frown.

'Oliver!' he harshly cried.
'Yes sir,' the poor boy said.
'Pull your cap from off your eyes,
And then hold up your head.'

Oliver did as he was asked
But with a massive sigh,
He covered his sad face and then
Began to cry and cry.

'Well!' exclaimed the beadle.
'You ungrateful little boy.
You are the worst disposed of lads
Or is this some new ploy?'

'No, no,' cried wretched Oliver.
'I will be good indeed.
I am a very little boy,
The only thing I need…'

'Is what?' cried the beadle.
His eyes were fierce and wild.
'I'm just so very lonely sir,'
Cried the desperate child.

'For everybody hates me.
Don't be cross with me.'
He beat his hand upon his heart
And cried in agony.

The beadle looked astonished;
He hemmed and hawed and said,
Something about a tickling cough,
Then shook his chubby head.

And then he took young Oliver
By the hand once more,
And walked in silence till they reached
The undertaker's door.

He entered without knocking.
Sowerberry sat there,
Making entries in a book
Which he did with great care.

'Aha,' he said, 'You're here at last.
Come in. Come in, right now.'
Bumble said, 'I've brought the boy.'
Oliver made a bow.

Sowerberry called his wife to come,
And then went on to add,
'Mr Bumble's here – he's brought
The little Workhouse lad.'

The undertaker's wife walked in.
She said, 'He's very small.
I do not like the look of him.
No really – not at all.'

Bumble said, 'He may be small
But one thing I do know,
For there is no denying it,
In time the boy will grow.'

'I'm sure he will,' the wife replied,
'But what I really think,
It will be 'cos he's feeding on
Our vittles and our drink.

'But husbands think they're always right,
Ignoring wifely moans,
So get downstairs you useless boy.
You little bag o' bones.'

As she spoke she opened up
A dingy wooden door.
A flight of stairs led down into
A cell with stone flagged floor.

'Twas dark and damp and cold in there.
The whole place reeked of gloom.
The coal cellar was just close by,
This was its ante-room .

It acted as the kitchen;
A young girl sat right there,
In shoes all down at heel and with
Long scruffy auburn hair.

Oliver was made to sit.
Mrs Sowerberry then said,
'Charlotte give the boy the bits
Intended to be fed…

'To Trip – for he ignored the scraps
We laid for him today.
I dare say boy you'd like some food,
I'm sure you wouldn't say…

'Your stomach's much too dainty
To eat these scraps of meat.'
Oliver insisted that
They'd be a welcome treat.

And yes they were – for meat was scarce
Where Oliver had been.
To see him eat was such a sight
As sad as any seen.

To watch him feed voraciously
Just like a hungry hog,
On bits of meat that had been left
To feed the mangy dog.

Once Oliver had finished
Each last fatty scrap,
Even bits that fell onto
His skinny little lap...

Mrs Sowerberry spoke out;
'I'll show you where you'll lie,
Beneath the counter in the shop –
Don't let me hear you cry.

'And I suppose you will not mind
Some company in there,
For you'll sleep with the coffins,
And if they give a scare...

'Well it's too bad – you have no choice,
There's nowhere else to sleep.'
So Oliver just followed her
With not the slightest peep.

Oliver spent a lonely night
And also we should tell,
A scary one, a spooky one,
A dismal one as well;

Surrounded by the shrouded shapes
Of coffins – forms of death.
They made him tremble deep inside
And took away his breath.

And deep regret engulfed his soul
That no good friend was there
To show some thought and kindliness
And maybe even care.

As he crept to his narrow bed
With no-one else around,
He wished it were his coffin,
To be placed in the ground…

Where he could calmly sleep at last
With gently waving grass
Above his head – where he could hear
A church bell made of brass…

Gently soothing him to sleep –
Oh what a lovely thought,
But all these cherished dreams of his
Just quickly came to naught.

For now it was the morning
And what a noise he heard.
He woke up with a sudden start
To see what had occurred.

It was a kicking sound and came
From on the outside door.
'Open up,' a voice yelled out,
And then the voice there swore.

Oliver cried, 'I will. I will.'
Time and time again.
He rushed to turn the heavy key
And to undo the chain.

'Yer the new boy ain't yer then?'
The voice from outside said.
'Yes,' said Oliver. Came reply
'I'll whop yer round the 'ead.

'Just wait until I get inside,
Yer little Work'us brat.'
Then he began to whistle
And ended their fraught chat.

Once the door was opened,
The voice's owner said,
'You don't know who I am Work'us?'
Oliver shook his head.

'I'm Mister Noah Claypole
And you are under me.'
And then he kicked poor Oliver
And caught him on the knee.

OLIVER GETS INTO A FIGHT

And so young Oliver began
His undertaker's life,
One filled with toil and trouble and
A deal of pain and strife.

For while he learnt this gruesome trade
Which he did not enjoy,
Noah Claypole pestered him;
He bullied the small boy.

He made his life a misery
And did it all the time;
The way that Claypole carried on
Was tantamount to crime.

Oliver was hardly fed,
The Sowerberrys saw to that;
They treated him with gross disdain
And called him just 'the brat'.

But following a month long trial
Sowerberry declared,
Oliver was apprenticed,
And said now this was squared…

The boy would lead processions,
Hat ribbons hanging down;
He'd head all of the funerals
They did around the town.

And how the mourners loved him.
It truly was the case
That everyone was quite bewitched
By his sweet mournful face.

And so young Oliver's hard life
Carried on this way,
Quite miserable and horrible,
Until one wretched day,

When Noah Claypole had come down
Into the kitchen there –
All sullenly demanding food
As he sank in a chair.

Oliver was there alone,
Afraid to thus be caught
By Claypole in a vicious mood,
Who had one single thought…

To aggravate the Work'us lad.
He always thought it fun
It whiled away an idle hour,
When all was said and done.

He taunted him and pulled his hair
And gave his nose a tweak,
And said he'd come and see him hang,
And said he was a sneak.

But Oliver did not react.
He didn't even sigh.
So Noah thought he'd push his luck
To make the poor lad cry.

'Work'us,' he said, 'yes I mean you,
And surely no-one other,
I've got a question for you now,
Tell me, 'ow's yer mother?'

Oliver cried out, 'She's dead.
Just leave it. Let it be.
And don't you dare say anything
About my mum to me.'

'What did she die of Work'us?'
Claypole kept on going.
'Or don't you have the slightest way
Of ever even knowing.'

Oliver spoke, more to himself,
As if he'd not impart
His inner feelings – but he breathed,
'Just from a broken heart.

'That's what an old nurse told me.
I think I truly know
What it's like to die from that.'
He held his head down low.

A tear ran gently down his cheek.
Claypole was set for more.
He shouted out in raucous voice,
'What yer snivelling for?'

Oliver was most upset;
Red faced and getting hot.
'Don't speak about my mum to me.
Claypole – you'd better not!'

'Better not,' Claypole exclaimed.
'Well! Better not for sure.
Yer mother was a nice 'un.
Oh yes she was. Oh lor!

'You know what Work'us – can't be helped,
I'm sorry for it too,
But yer old mother really was
A bad 'un through and through.'

'What did you say?' cried Oliver.
'I said,' Claypole replied,
'She was a bad 'un that's for sure.
It's better that she died,

'Else she'd be there hard labouring.
Transported – maybe hung.'
Oliver in fury cried,
'Claypole – hold your tongue.'

He threw the chair and table
Completely out the way,
Seized Claypole by his mangy throat
And he began to spray…

Claypole with a range of blows
That made a crunching sound,
Until with one almighty punch
He felled him to the ground.

Oliver was now transformed,
His spirit roused at last.
Manly anger came in waves
Both thick and very fast.

The insult to his mother,
Despicable and dire,
Had changed his personality
And set his blood on fire.

No longer meek and quiet
Like the lad of old,
His eyes were bright and vivid,
He stood erect and bold.

He stared at Noah Claypole –
His tormentor – who now lay
Crouching at his feet and in
A very cowardly way.

Claypole cried out desperately,
'He'll murder me for sure.'
His cries brought Mrs Sowerberry
And Charlotte to the door.

They grabbed riled Oliver with force
And kicked and pummelled him.
Their punches landed on his chest,
His face and every limb.

Noah Claypole roused himself
And punched the boy as well,
And then they dragged poor Oliver
Into a dusty cell.

'Twas the cellar where he went.
They locked the wooden door.
'There, there, Noah,' Charlotte said.
'He'll trouble you no more.'

Mrs Sowerberry sank down,
Full of dreadful fears,
Into a chair and then she burst
Into a flood of tears.

'What's to be done?' she cried aloud.
'He'll break the cellar door.
With all that kicking it'll break,
In minutes – not much more.'

'And Mr Sowerberry's away.
Whatever shall we do?'
And then a thought flashed through her mind
Of somebody she knew.

'Noah, you must run right now
To Mr Bumble for
He'll know what we should do – and yes
He'll sort it out for sure.

'Don't lose a minute, tell him this –
He must come right away.
Tell him it's most important and
There must be no delay.'

So Noah set off rapidly –
The beadle, without doubt,
Was the man to handle things
And sort the whole mess out.

'AIN'T YOU A-TREMBLIN' OLIVER?'

When Claypole reached the Workhouse,
He found the beadle there;
He shouted out and carried on
And made old Bumble stare.

He cried out in an urgent voice,
'Oh, Mr Bumble sir.
It's Oliver – he's turned into
A mean and vicious cur.

'He tried to murder me and then
He tried to kill the missis,
And then he threatened Charlotte;
Oh, what a fine mess this is.

'He's running wild and crazy.
I think he's going mad.
I tell you Mr Bumble
Things is really bad.'

The beadle puffed himself right up.
He took his hat and cane,
Adjusted them to sit just right,
To make it very plain…

That he was on a mission,
A beadle in control.
'I'll take care of this,' he cried.
'Come on – let's take a stroll.'

They went back to the funeral shop
To see what was the score,
And found that Oliver still raged
Against the cellar door.

Bumble thought it would be wise
To parley for a while,
He didn't like young Oliver's
New found aggressive style.

And so he called out, 'Oliver!
Do you know this 'ere voice?
You can behave or pay the price.
You have, my lad, a choice.'

'I know just who you are all right.'
The boy's response was made
With no fear – and Bumble cried,
'Good Lord – ain't you afraid.

'Ain't you a-trembling while I speak?'
Bold Oliver cried, 'No!'
Bumble was astounded by
This unrepentant show.

Mrs Sowerberry wrung her hands
And shook her weary head.
'How could he speak to you like that?
He must be mad,' she said.

'No he's not mad,' the beadle breathed.
He looked down at his feet.
He thought for just a moment then
He sighed, 'It's down to meat!'

Mrs Sowerberry was shocked
And Bumble shook his head.
'You've been too generous by half.
The boy's been overfed.

'You've fed the boy on scraps of meat.'
Bumble's tone was stern.
'I've seen it all before – oh yes,
For I can now discern…

'You've raised an artificial soul,
A spirit in the lad
That's unbecoming – not quite right,
Unusual and plain bad.

'I tell you very clearly ma'am
And don't mean to be cruel,
This never would have happened if
You'd kept the boy on gruel.'

Mrs Sowerberry raised her eyes.
She said, 'Oh deary dear.
This comes of being liberal
And kindly too, I fear.'

She revelled in her piousness,
A quite amazing feat,
For all she'd given Oliver
Was food no-one would eat.

Bumble looked at her and said,
'There's but one thing to do.
Just leave him in the cellar now
For a day or two.

'Leave him there until you're sure
He is half starved – then ma'am,
Feed him just a little gruel
For this will do no harm'

But then – Mr Sowerberry
Came back and quickly saw
How things stood – and then he said,
'Open the cellar door.'

And in a twinkling, out he dragged
The poor boy by the collar.
'Now you're a nice 'un, ain't you?'
He was heard to holler.

Oliver came tumbling out,
His face was scratched and bruised,
So it was clear to Sowerberry
That he'd been badly used.

'He called my mother awful names.'
The boy's tone was still terse.
Mrs Sowerberry said, 'So what!
She earned it – and much worse'

'She didn't,' cried poor Oliver.
'It's all a dreadful lie.'
Mrs Sowerberry yelled, 'It's not.'
And she began to cry.

Sowerberry then cuffed the boy,
More to appease his wife,
Yet he felt some small sympathy
For Oliver's harsh life.

And so he shut the boy up in
The kitchen now instead.
Then later when the sun went down
Told him to go to bed.

OLIVER'S ESCAPE

When Oliver was left alone
Amid the dreadful gloom
Of his eerie resting place –
The scary workshop room –

His feelings just gave way and we
I'm sure can fathom why;
He fell onto the floor and then
Once more began to cry.

While he'd been under their attacks
He'd done so much to hide
How he felt – he had not sobbed –
And purely out of pride.

But now he was a boy again;
A little child alone.
Resigned but deeply torn apart
At being on his own.

He lay there motionless for hours,
For how long just God knows,
But then, quite cautiously at first,
He shook himself and rose,

And gently then he slid the catch
And opened up the door;
On looking out he was entranced
And moved by what he saw.

The night was cold and dark as pitch,
But what a lovely sight,
For there to see – so high above –
On that chill, moonlit night…

The heavens were alive with stars,
A sight of priceless worth;
To his young eyes they seemed to be
Much further from the Earth…

Than he had ever seen before;
No trace of wind there blew,
The world looked death-like, strange and still
And wore a sombre hue.

He softly closed the door and by
The fast expiring light
Of the candle – tied his things
Most carefully and tight…

Inside a dirty handkerchief,
Then stifling a yawn,
He sat upon a wooden bench
To wait the break of dawn.

When faltering, grey rays of light
Fell on the stony floor,
Oliver rose gingerly –
Once more unbarred the door.

He looked to left and right and spied
That all was calm and still:
There was no-one around and so
He set off up the hill.

He took the route he'd walked along
When he'd left Mrs Mann.
He had no sense of where to go
And no coherent plan.

He wandered on and then he found
He was now right outside
The little children's Parish house
Where under-eights reside.

And though it was still early,
The chill was now receding;
He saw a little child was in
The garden, gamely weeding.

It was a younger, former friend
With whom he'd often got
Into hot water – yes indeed,
They'd really shared a lot.

For they'd been starved together
And beaten often too,
And shut up in a cellar
With not a thing to do.

Side by side they'd suffered,
Such trials without end,
So Oliver was very pleased
To see his former friend.

The little boy ran to the gate
In an excited rush.
Oliver whispered frantically,
'Careful Dick. Please hush.

'Is anybody up just yet?'
He looked around to see.
The little boy just shook his head.
'Nobody's up but me.'

'You mustn't say you saw me Dick.
I plan to run away.
They've beaten and ill-used me,
And so this very day…

'I'm off to seek my fortune;
I don't know where I'll go,
But I will never come back here,
That is one thing I know.

'But little Dick – how pale you are,'
Oliver said sighing.
Dick coughed, 'I heard the doctor say
He thought that I was dying.

'But oh, I am so very glad
To see you here my dear,
But do not stop – for if you do
You may be caught, I fear.'

'Yes. Yes. I'll say goodbye to you,'
Oliver softly said.
'I know we'll meet again sometime.'
Young Dick there shook his head.

'I hope we do,' he sadly sighed.
'When we are dead I'm sure.
I know the doctor must be right,
So it won't be before.

'I dream of heaven all the time
And see for mercy's sake,
Angels and kind faces that
I don't see when awake.

'Kiss me,' cried the little child.
He climbed onto the gate.
He flung his arms round Oliver,
Now in a sorry state.

'Goodbye my dear. God bless you,'
He cried through flowing tears.
This blessing from a young child's lips
Was first in all the years…

That Oliver had ever heard
Invoked upon his head,
And through the strife and suffering
Wherever his life led…

Across the endless years to come,
And in all kinds of strife,
'Twas one he never once forgot
Throughout his later life.

THE ARTFUL DODGER

By eight o'clock that morning
Oliver had covered
A good five miles but still he feared
That he might be discovered.

He feared that he might be pursued;
They'd come and drag him back,
And so he pushed himself – he thought
He shouldn't rest or slack.

But finally he took a pause
And gratefully sat down
By a milestone which announced
That famous London town…

Was seventy long miles away –
But Oliver still thought
That London could ensure that he
Avoided being caught.

For finding him would be just like
Hunting for a needle.
No-one would ever catch him there,
Not even that fat beadle.

And he'd heard others often say
It surely was the case,
That there were opportunities
In that exciting place.

And so it was decided,
He'd head for London town,
And put some miles behind him
Before the sun went down.

He had a crust of bread, a shirt,
Stockings – nothing more –
Wrapped in his little bundle, plus
The scruffy clothes he wore.

And a penny, Sowerberry
Had given him one day –
Following a funeral –
As a means to say…

That he was specially happy;
It was a way to tell
Young Oliver that he was pleased –
The boy had acted well.

And that was it, small help he thought
For such a lengthy walk,
So stoically he gave himself
An earnest, little talk.

And then he trudged towards his goal.
Up hills, through vales, o'er stiles.
And on that first day on the road,
He covered twenty miles.

And when the darkness fell he crept
With aching legs and back,
Into the shelter offered by
A towering haystack.

He was worn out and hungry
And fell there in a heap,
And being tired from walking
He soon fell fast asleep.

When he awoke he felt so cold,
Hungry and half dead,
So spent his only penny on
A little loaf of bread.

He struggled on with weary legs.
His feet were raw and sore.
By close of day he'd only walked
Twelve miles – for sure, no more.

He spent another freezing night
Just huddled outside there.
A tiny ball of misery
Out in the damp, bleak air.

Next morning he then waited at
The bottom of a hill:
He stood alone there shivering –
But patiently – until…

A stagecoach came along and then
He begged the folk on board,
'Please can you spare me anything?'
At first he was ignored,

But then some of the passengers
Said, 'Tell you what my lad,
Run up the hill beside the coach,
Keep up and then by gad,

'We'll give you half a penny,
If it is properly done.'
So Oliver, most wearily
Began to gamely run.

But he soon fell behind and so
The people laughed and jeered,
They yelled he hadn't tried enough –
Their money disappeared,

And they declared he was indeed,
An idle, feckless dog,
And then they disappeared into
A cloud of dusty smog.

So painfully he carried on,
Beaten down and cowed:
Some places had large signs that said
No begging was allowed.

The penalty was clearly shown –
They said that without fail,
Anyone caught begging there
Would do a term in jail.

So Oliver received scant help,
For most folk's passing whim
Was to tell him to 'Clear orf.'
Or set their dog on him.

And truly if it hadn't been
For an old lady and
A turnpike man who both had lent
The lad a helping hand…

He likely would have starved to death,
Or something just as bad,
And had the sort of sorry end
That his poor mother had.

They'd handed him a bite to eat,
And this most welcome food
Had given strength – and lightened too
His downcast, sorry mood.

'Twas after being on the road
For seven long hard days,
That Oliver, one morning,
Saw there within his gaze…

A sign that said he'd travelled to
The town of Barnet where,
The folk were very proud because
Of Barnet's famous fair.

And he was sure he was now close
To sprawling London town,
And with this thought he sighed and then
Just sat himself right down.

He chose a step on which to rest,
Then took a look about:
It was a busy little place,
Of that there was no doubt.

He watched the people walking by,
Up and through the town,
And then he saw a funny lad
Who looked him up and down.

It was a boy about his age
Who held him with a stare.
Quite unconcerned he might seem rude
As he stood staring there.

Oliver returned his gaze
With furrowed, crinkled brow.
And then the boy walked over
And said, 'Now what's the row?'

He was the very queerest boy.
Whatever did he mean?
Yes, quite the strangest looking lad
That Oliver had seen.

With low, flat brow and squat, snub nose
And common in the face,
And dirty as a juvenile
Had ever been the case.

And for his age he was quite short,
His small and childish size
Did not affect his confidence;
His sharp and ugly eyes…

Darted round – saw everything,
And anyone would say
He had a very swaggering
And cocky kind of way.

His hat was stuck upon his head,
So lightly there and all,
It seemed at any moment
It might come loose and fall.

This would have likely happened
If he'd not had the knack
Of giving his small head a twitch
To put the hat right back.

He wore a grown man's overcoat
That reached down to his feet;
It was so long it trailed behind
And dragged along the street.

So there he stood, a likely lad,
Just looking on – deadpan –
With all the airs and graces and
The manners of a man.

'Hello my covey! What's the row?'
He spoke out once again.
Oliver then answered though
The question wasn't plain.

'I'm very tired and hungry.
I've walked for seven days.
Down highways and down dusty lanes
And lonely, small byways.'

'For sivin days,' the young gent cried.
'My eyes – well, you'll want grub.
We'll get some ham and bread and then
Some beer from that there pub.'

And it was very quickly done
And Oliver then ate.
My how those ham rolls tasted good.
They really were first rate.

'Going down to London then?'
The strange boy smugly said.
'Yes,' replied young Oliver.
'Where will you lay your head?'

'I've no idea,' sighed Oliver.
The lad said, 'Never fear.
I can help you out – relax,
And just enjoy your beer,

'For down in London town, I know
Someone who surely can
Help you out and all for nowt –
A kindly gentleman.

'He'll give you lodgings, that he will,
Because he always shows
His kindly side if introduced
By someone that he knows.

'And don't he know me – not at all –
Not in the least,' he said.
He smiled to show his irony
And smugly shook his head.

The offer of some shelter
Was welcome – yes indeed;
So Oliver accepted,
And after his small feed…

He talked some more with his new friend,
Who told him that his name
Was Jack Dawkins – but his friends,
By way of a fun game…

Called him 'The artful Dodger'.
A strange name that's for sure.
But Oliver accepted it
And then said nothing more.

OLIVER MEETS A KINDLY OLD GENTLEMAN

The Dodger wouldn't entertain
Reaching London town,
Not until the sun had set,
And was completely down;

And so it very nearly was
Eleven by the time
They entered London's darkened streets,
Alive with crime and grime.

They crossed the 'pike at Islington,
Then into St. John's Road,
Past Sadler's Wells and Coppice Row –
Still on the Dodger strode.

Across the ground that once was known
As Hockley-in-the Hole.
To Saffron Hill – thought Oliver,
'What is our final goal?'

Now they were walking through some streets
That Oliver could see
Were just about as dirty as
A place could ever be.

The streets were filthy, grimy,
With nasty odours there,
And drunken men and women
Were lounging everywhere.

This surely was the kind of place
It would be best to shun,
So Oliver began to think
It might be best to run.

Just disappear while there was still
A chance to get away,
But Dodger knocked upon a door
And he heard someone say…

'Now then – let's be having it.'
Dodger leant towards the door.
'Plummy and slam,' he whispered.
The other voice then swore.

This was the strangest thing of all
That Oliver had heard,
But he assumed it must be just
Some kind of crude password.

The dingy door was opened.
A pale face then peeped out.
'There's two of you,' he fiercely cried.
'So what's this all about?

'Wherever did he come from then?'
He shook his dirty head.
The Dodger faced him fair and square.
'Greenland!' he tersely said.

'So where's old Fagin – up the stairs?
And cut your snipes and gripes.'
The face replied, 'He's sortin' out
The latest batch of wipes.'

So up some broken stairs they went
Into a dirty room
That had a really dismal feel
And special kind of gloom.

There was a meagre, feeble fire
And a single candle.
A frying pan was on the hob,
And its burnt out old handle…

Was held in place by shabby string,
And sizzling in the pan
Were sausages – attended by
A shrivelled up old man.

He stood there with a toasting fork.
He had an evil stare;
A quite repulsive looking face
And with red, matted hair.

White, mangy skin with wrinkled brow
And pasty, haggard hue,
His countenance held such a look
That chilled all those he knew.

He wore a greasy, flannel gown.
His wiry throat was bare,
And while he fried the sausages
He gazed with tender care…

At some fine, silk handkerchiefs,
That had been washed and wrung,
Then placed upon a clothes horse where
They all now neatly hung.

And seated round a table
There was a motley crowd
Of boys about the Dodger's age,
All confident and proud,

And cocky too – for it was clear
That as they sat there then,
They all adopted quite the air
Of middle-aged fine men.

For each one smoked a long clay pipe
And drank a spot of gin.
They all looked up as the old man
Turned round with wily grin.

'See what I've found.' The Dodger
Pulled Oliver by the wrist.
'Yes Fagin, here he is, he's called
Mister Oliver Twist.'

The old man with contrivance,
Made a long, low bow,
His face – contorted in a smile –
Looked almost friendly now.

'I hope to have the honour of,'
His voice rose up and fell,
'Your intimate acquaintance – yes –
To get to know you well.'

Once he had said these kindly words
The others gathered round
And shook him firmly by the hand
And said that they were bound…

To say it was a pleasure
And a 'onour too,
To make his fine acquaintance and
To say how do ye do?

They checked his little bundle
And rifled then as well
Through his pockets – everywhere,
And had the cheek to tell…

Poor Oliver they did it,
Because they knew for sure
He'd be too tired to empty them,
And this was why, they swore…

They were just being helpful,
He shouldn't take offence.
It was a friendly thing to do,
They said in their defence.

But anyway, their actions
And their idle talk,
Were soon put to an end and by
The old man's toasting fork.

He struck them on their shoulders
And on their heads as well,
And said, 'We're glad dear Oliver,
If truth we are to tell…

'To see you in our humble home.
Oh yes, we are indeed.
Now Dodger, get some sausages –
The boy will want to feed.

'And draw a crate up to the fire.
There, that's right, my dear.
You'll need to warm yourself and so
It's best to pull it near.'

And then the old man noticed
Oliver's eyes had turned,
Towards the hanging handkerchiefs.
He said, 'Ha, you've discerned…

'We're busy washing handkerchiefs.
We do it with such care –
And there's so many of them,
My dear, a-hanging there.'

All the boys laughed heartily
As the old man spoke.
They obviously were in the know
On some insiders joke.

Oliver ate his sausages –
The old man, with a grin,
Said, 'Drink this up – and quickly,'
And gave him some hot gin.

Then in an instant, Oliver
Collapsed into a heap,
And very quickly after that
He was quite sound asleep.

FAGIN'S TREASURE

When Oliver awoke next day
He saw the wizened man
Boiling coffee on the fire
In an old saucepan.

Though Oliver had roused himself,
And with a little shake,
He still was in that drowsy place,
Not fully wide awake.

He lay there prone and motionless,
And didn't make a peep,
And yet aware of everything –
Although he seemed asleep.

Old Fagin stirred the coffee
And then he looked around,
And then he stared at Oliver
Who didn't make a sound.

And then old Fagin called his name;
'Oliver,' he said.
Then satisfied the boy there slept
He nodded his old head,

And bending over, opened up
In the wooden floor
What seemed to be to Oliver
Some kind of old trapdoor.

And from it Fagin pulled a box
And dragged it to a chair,
And opened it with glistening eyes
And with a greedy stare.

And then he took from in the box
All kinds of lovely things.
Bracelets, brooches, jewellery,
Gold watches, precious rings.

'Aha,' he sighed. 'Such clever dogs,
And everyone there swung,
And never peached on Fagin – no –
Just before they hung.

'And it's so good for trade and all,
Now they've all disappeared.
No-one to share the booty with –
No need to be afeard.'

As he spoke, his shining eyes,
All bright and almost black,
Looked up and then across the room –
Oliver stared back.

Their gaze met for a second.
Fagin was unnerved,
For he saw in an instant
That he had been observed.

Young Oliver had seen it all –
His precious, priceless stash.
He started up and closed the box
With an almighty crash.

Then furiously he made a grab
For the sharp bread knife.
'What have you seen?' he shouted out.
'Quick now. To save your life.

'Why are you wide awake, and what
Do you watch me for?'
My goodness how he carried on,
And waved the knife and swore.

Scared Oliver looked up and said,
Emotions all astir,
'I couldn't sleep for longer.
I'm very sorry sir.'

'Were you awake an hour ago?'
Fagin fiercely cried.
'Upon my word, I was asleep,'
Oliver replied.

'Tush, tush, my dear,' the old man said.
'Of course, I know that dear.
I only tried to frighten you.
You have no cause to fear.'

He played around now with the knife
As if he had been caught
Just in a little bit of fun
That was but idle sport.

'You're a brave boy, Oliver.
Now tell me then, my dear,
Did you see all those pretty things?'
He cocked his ear to hear.

'Yes sir, I did,' said Oliver.
Old Fagin then turned pale.
His worried mind now conjured up
The inside of a jail.

'They're just my little property,
For they are but the wage
I've earned through life, to live upon
In challenging old age.

'Some say I am a miser.'
He crinkled up his face.
Oliver thought, 'He surely is
To live in such a place…

'For he's got all those watches
And could afford to be
In somewhere nice and living
A life of luxury.'

Then Oliver just looked away
From where the trinkets shone,
And when his gaze returned, the box
With Fagin's stash was gone;

For in the blinking of an eye
Old Fagin, that sly fox,
Had scooped his treasure up and had
Concealed his precious box.

OLIVER LEARNS A NEW TRADE

Shortly after this exchange
The Dodger came on back.
He brought with him hot rolls and ham
To make a breakfast snack.

Another lad who'd been there too,
On the night before,
Came in with Dodger, and then once
They had secured the door…

He was led to Oliver.
His name was Charley Bates.
'Pleased to meet you,' Charley grinned,
As they sat down on crates.

'Well, my dears,' old Fagin said,
'I know you wouldn't shirk,
So tell me boys that you've both been
Out there and hard at work.'

'Yes, hard,' replied the Dodger.
'As nails,' bold Charley said.
'Good boys. Good boys,' the old man laughed,
And nodded his bent head.

'What have you got then Dodger?'
'Two wallets,' he replied.
He brought out two – one red, one green –
Made of the finest hide.

'Ain't they lovely Fagin.
So lovely and refined.'
The old man screwed his face and said,
'Yes – but are they lined?'

'Pretty well,' the Dodger said.
'Could be better,' Fagin sighed.
'But very neat and nicely made.'
Then turning to the side…

He spoke to Oliver and said
With a loathsome leer,
'Ingenious workman, ain't he?
Don't you agree, my dear?'

'Indeed I do,' said Oliver.
Charley laughed with glee.
Oliver was quite bemused
Because he failed to see…

What in the world was funny.
He turned a little red.
Fagin laughed, 'What's that you've got?'
'Some wipes,' young Charley said.

Fagin picked them up and then
He closely checked them out.
He said, 'They're very good ones too,
Of that there is no doubt.

'Oliver, I'm sure you'd wish
To be like Charley here,
In making handkerchiefs with ease –
Wouldn't you my dear?'

Oliver said, 'Oh, yes I would.
If you will teach me sir.'
Charley Bates just fell about
And nearly did incur…

A bout of suffocation.
He laughed so very much.
He said, 'I've never in my life
Heard the likes of such.'

When he had quite recovered,
He said, 'I've never seen
Anyone in all my life
Who really is so green.'

Oliver sat wondering
How they had found the time
To be industrious in this way –
He never thought of crime!

And then right after breakfast
They played a funny game,
And Oliver just didn't grasp
Exactly its real aim.

It was performed in this strange way –
The merry gentleman
Stood erect and serious,
His face set and deadpan,

Then he placed a silver snuff box
In his trouser pocket,
And then around his neck he hung
A lovely chain and locket.

Into his waistcoat he then slipped
A silver watch and chain;
Placed 'kerchiefs in his coat, then took
A sturdy, wooden cane…

Then trotted up and down the room
In that peculiar way,
That gentlemen parade the streets
Each and every day.

He'd stop right by the fireplace
And sometimes at the door,
He looked ahead with that rapt stare
That earnest shoppers wore.

And then he looked around and checked
On his handkerchief,
Clearly making sure he'd not
Been caught out by a thief.

He'd slap his pocket with his hand
To allay his fears
That something had been stolen:
Oliver shed tears…

For it was very funny,
He laughed so much he cried,
And all the time the boys were there,
By Fagin – at his side…

Keeping close, but dodging
If Fagin should turn round.
Furtively they followed him
And didn't make a sound.

At last the Dodger stepped upon
His toes – and in a flash,
Charley stumbled into him
And then the old gent's stash…

Of jewellery and everything
Was taken in a trice.
Their actions were so swift and deft,
Clever and precise.

They lifted from the old man's clothes
The snuff box, watch and chain,
And other things, and then they did
The whole thing once again.

In fact they did it many times.
Each time it was the same,
And Oliver looked on and thought
It was the strangest game.

And then two visitors arrived.
Two ladies strolled right in.
They had long hair, quite badly combed,
And ruddy coloured skin.

They weren't exactly pretty
But looked quite stout and hearty,
As if they were the types who would
Enjoy a rowdy party.

Oliver thought them very nice,
As they both were, no doubt.
One was Nancy, t'other Bet –
And they'd been round about…

And thought they'd make a call upon
The fine, young gentlemen,
And so they'd made their way unto
Old Fagin's grimy den.

It didn't take that long at all
For liquor to appear,
And everyone grew boisterous,
Full of goodwill and cheer.

Then Charley Bates stood up and said
Quite serious and aloof,
'I think the time has come for us
To go and pad the hoof.'

Young Oliver was most perplexed
As he sat on his bench.
He thought this must mean 'going out',
Or something else in French.

Then Charley and the Dodger,
And the ladies too,
Went out and left young Oliver
With nothing much to do.

'There, there my dear,' said Fagin,
In his creepy way.
'Such a pleasant life they have –
They've gone out for the day.'

'So have they finished working now?'
Oliver enquired.
'Yes,' said Fagin knowingly.
'But they may be required…

'To do a little if a job
Should unexpectedly
Come across their path – well then
They'll tend to it, you see.

'They won't neglect it that's for sure.'
He spoke with laughing sneer,
And tapped his shovel on the hearth,
'Make 'em your models dear.

'Do everything they ask of you.
Attend to their fine way.
Especially to the Dodger for –
I'd be so bold to say…

'One day he'll be a famous man,
And he'll make you one too,
That's if you follow everything
That Dodger bids you do.

'Now is my handkerchief, by chance,'
He said with slimy leer,
'A-hanging from my pocket there.
Now can you see it dear?'

'Yes it is,' said Oliver.
'It's large and blue and red.'
'Well, see if you can take it out –
But softly,' Fagin said.

'And in a way that makes quite sure
I'm really not aware.
Just like you saw the others do.'
So Oliver with care…

Held the pocket with one hand
And drew the handkerchief,
Not knowing he was being trained
To soon become a thief.

'Is it gone?' old Fagin cried,
All innocent and bland.
'Here it is,' called Oliver
Holding out his hand.

'Oh, you're a clever boy, my dear,'
The old man slyly said,
And patted Oliver three times
Upon his upturned head.

'I never saw a sharper lad,
So take this shilling here,
For if you carry on this way
I promise you, my dear…

'You'll be the greatest man of all.'
But Oliver just thought,
How could this come about and from
What he had just been taught?

For how could picking pockets make
A great man out of him?
It seemed so strange and surely was
Merely the old man's whim.

But then he thought the gentleman
Must certainly be blest,
With knowledge and intelligence
And therefore must know best.

OLIVER GOES TO WORK WITH THE DODGER

For many days young Oliver
Practised all the time,
Quite unaware that he prepared
For a life of crime.

But then he grew so very tired
Cooped up in the gloom
In Fagin's dank, depressing
Airless, dismal room.

So he began to languish
And yearn for cool, fresh air,
And asked the bent, old gentleman
If he might go and share…

The opportunity to work –
Not be an idle lodger.
To go and toil with Charley Bates
And with the artful Dodger.

He was encouraged to this view,
For he could clearly see,
Fagin's wicked character
And stern morality.

For if he thought the boys inclined
To avoid their work;
If he was tempted to the view
That they were wont to shirk;

And if they came back there at night
Completely empty-handed,
Fagin's comments would be fierce,
Violent, cruel and candid.

For he'd go on and horribly,
His foul words running rife
About the consequences of
An idle, lazy life.

And then to really force the point
Of everything he'd said,
He'd cuff the boys and send them off
Quite supperless to bed.

Then finally, one morning
Fagin said, 'Okay.'
He told the eager Oliver
He could now have his way.

'Go with Bates and Dodger:
Watch everything they do.
You'll be under their tuition,
They'll both look after you.'

And so they sallied forth, they were
A quite peculiar sight.
The Dodger had his sleeves tucked up
And hat cocked to the right.

And Charley Bates, he sauntered on
Hands in pockets – thus
They made their way with confidence
And with no fear or fuss.

And Oliver was very keen
To now become well versed
In making lovely handkerchiefs,
And thought, 'What will come first?

'What area of making them
Will they both show me now?'
But looking on he was amazed,
It furrowed his small brow;

For now it all became quite clear,
Their purpose there and then –
Was to steal and thus deceive
Old, unsuspecting men.

For Dodger made a sudden stop.
Oliver asked why.
Dodger laid his finger on
His lips, and with a sigh…

He whispered, 'Hush now Oliver.
Don't make a sound at all.
Now do you see that old cove by
The second hand bookstall?'

Oliver replied he did.
'He'll do,' the Dodger said.
'A first class plant,' laughed Charley Bates.
As the old man stood and read.

Oliver looked at the pair
And watched them as they went,
Across the road and then towards
The smartly dressed old gent.

He had a powdered head and wore
Glasses made of gold;
A bottle-green, smart overcoat –
Protection from the cold.

And trousers that were creamy white,
Well tailored yet quite plain,
And in his hand he tightly held
A lovely, bamboo cane.

He'd chosen from the bookstall
The book which he now read
With total concentration and
A bowed and studied head.

And he was quite oblivious
To everything around,
As Charley and the Dodger
Approached without a sound.

Oliver stood watching
With wide-eyed, rapt surprise,
And then his jaw dropped open
And horror filled his eyes.

For now he saw the Dodger
Plunge his hand into
The gentleman's coat pocket,
And then bring into view…

A handkerchief of finest silk,
And once this had been done,
He handed it to Charley Bates
And they began to run.

And now it dawned on Oliver,
He saw it all at once
And realised he'd been a fool,
Too trusting and a dunce.

The mystery of the handkerchiefs,
The watches – all the gear,
Now made sound sense and in a flash
It all became quite clear.

The revelation hit him –
How they had been so cunning.
He stood for just a moment, then
He also set off running…

For now he was quite terrified.
He ran he knew not where.
His only object now was just
To get away from there.

But then as he began to run
The old man went to draw
His 'kerchief from his pocket,
And in an instant saw…

It wasn't there and also then
He spied the running lad;
So when he saw him scudding off
He cried aloud, 'By gad,

'I do believe that wicked boy
Has got my handkerchief.'
He set off chasing after him,
And cried, 'Quick, stop that thief.'

And sadly I must here recount
He wasn't on his own
In chasing after Oliver –
No, he was not alone.

For Charley Bates and Dodger,
To avoid attention,
Or something worse, like being caught
And placed then in detention…

Dodged into a doorway
To avoid such grief,
Then issued forth with promptitude
And shouted out, 'Stop thief!'

And so the angry gentleman
And two he'd once called 'friend',
Chased Oliver along the street:
He did his best to wend…

In and out of obstacles –
He felt he was destined
To spend some time in prison so –
He ran just like the wind.

But there is intrigue in the sound
Of people calling out,
'Stop thief. Stop thief.' It surely is
A most distinctive shout.

It made the busy tradesmen
Leave what they were doing,
Intent on finding out just what
In the world was brewing.

The butcher threw his tray away;
The milkman dropped his pail.
The errand-boy his parcels,
And every angry male…

Now joined in hot pursuit and ran
A-shouting down the street,
And soon there were a hundred pairs
Of pounding, dashing feet.

And on they run, pell-mell they go.
Helter-skelter, screaming,
Through the tangled streets and down
The alley ways a-teeming.

Knocking down pedestrians,
Rousing up the dogs.
Scruffy people, many more –
In their smartest togs.

Scaring chickens, bearing on
And growing all the time,
Combined to make a robber pay
For his foul, wicked crime.

Up go windows, people shout.
The voices join as one.
'Stop the thief. Stop the thief.'
And on the rabble run.

There seems to be a passion
That turns a mob quite wild,
And in this case they just pursued
One wretched, breathless child.

He panted with exhaustion.
His eyes were open wide,
Doing all he could to find
A sheltered place to hide.

But then it's over suddenly,
A clever, nasty blow –
He's on the pavement – everyone
Gathers round to crow.

They want to look, to ogle him,
Then someone standing there
Says, 'Stand aside. Stand aside.
Give the lad some air.'

Another with a stony heart,
Unpleasantly observes,
'You're speaking utter nonsense.
It's not what he deserves.'

Then someone else with raucous shout
Cried, 'Come on now. Make way.
Here comes the ill-used gentleman.
Right now, my lad, you'll pay.'

And then the gentleman approached.
'Is this the boy?' they said.
The old man looked at Oliver
And sadly bowed his head.

For Oliver lay in the dust
And he was smeared with mud,
And his poor, frightened, wretched face
Was covered all in blood.

The gentleman replied and said,
'Yes, I'm afraid to say
That this is him.' He faced towards
The pushing, baying fray.

And they responded laughingly.
'Afraid!' they cried as one.
'Afraid he says and after what
This lad 'as bin and done.'

But the gentleman was kindly.
His face was soft and mellow.
'I fear that he has hurt himself.
The poor, young, wretched fellow.'

'I did that to 'im' – a lout
Said with a cocky chuckle.
'I 'it 'im in the mouth real 'ard.
See 'ere, I cut me knuckle.'

He touched his hat, he wore a grin,
Cheeky, proud and broad.
The gentleman could see that he
Expected a reward.

He looked at him with deep disgust
And then he turned away,
For now a policeman had arrived
And he had heard him say…

'Get up, get up you little rogue.
You thieving little cur.'
Oliver cried, 'It wasn't me.
It was two others sir.'

He looked around and then exclaimed,
'I saw them standing here.'
But they'd already taken steps
To get away and clear.

Dodger and smart Charley
Knew better than to dally,
They'd fled off down – with mounting speed –
The first convenient alley.

'Come on, get up,' the policeman yelled.
His manner was most grim.
The kindly gentleman spoke out.
'Take care and don't hurt him.'

The policeman laughed, 'What hurt him now.
Oh no, the thieving cheat.'
And then he pulled poor Oliver
Roughly to his feet.

The boy was in an awful state
For he could hardly stand.
The policeman grabbed his collar
With one enormous hand.

He dragged him down the heaving street
And at a rapid pace.
The gentleman now followed too,
Concern upon his face.

The crowd all came along as well.
They shouted out and stared.
And in amongst it all, a boy,
Alone, confused and scared.

THE MAGISTRATE

Now Oliver was taken to
A grim, run-down police station,
About as dark and dirty as
Any in the nation.

And he was thrown into a cell,
In such a bloodied state,
There to await his time before
The awful magistrate.

The gentleman now waited too
And as he did, he thought
About the young boy waiting there
To go before the court.

'There's something quite familiar
About that young lad's face.
I feel I've seen it somewhere else
But it's so hard to place.

'God bless my soul,' he pondered,
His chin pressed on his book.
'I do believe I've seen before
That faraway, soft look.'

He trawled his mind for someone
Who looked the very same.
Searching through his brain to find
A face, a look, a name.

He thought of friends and then of foes,
Of faces from the past.
Then finally he shook his head,
Giving up at last.

He turned back to his book to wait
For the court to start,
And though he read, still he felt
A pounding in his heart.

For something 'bout the little boy
Had touched his very soul,
And now to see him free and well
Became his only goal.

He was summoned then, at last
Into an office where
The magistrate – a Mr Fang
Sat in his sturdy chair.

Fang had a reputation
That told his every mood
Was angry, crass, unpleasant,
Bad-tempered – just plain rude.

When the gentleman walked in
He said, 'So who are you?'
The old man handed him his card.
Fang grabbed it and then threw…

The card away and with contempt,
And then was heard to bellow,
'Officer, step up and tell
Who is this ancient fellow?'

'My name, good sir, is Brownlow.
And may I now enquire
The name of such a magistrate
Whose rude words do conspire…

'To insult a gentleman?
It really will not do.'
Fang looked down with utter scorn,
Appearing in a stew.

He stared across at Brownlow,
His glare as hard as rock,
It seemed he thought this old man was
The felon in the dock.

'What's the charge against this man?'
The officer then said;
'He's not charged, your worship,'
(Brownlow's face turned red.)

'He appears against this boy.'
He motioned to his side.
'Well swear him in and quickly,'
The monstrous Fang replied.

'Before I'm sworn,' Brownlow exclaimed,
'I'd like to say a word,
For I would never have believed
What has now just occurred.'

'Hold your tongue sir,' Fang yelled out.
'I'll not,' Brownlow replied.
Fang cried, 'If you don't hold your tongue
You will be thrown outside.'

Oh my, how he got all worked up.
Really in a state.
He cried, 'How dare you bully
The Crown's own magistrate.

'Swear him in. Swear him in.
I won't hear any more.'
So Mr Brownlow took the stand
And dutifully he swore.

And then he tried to tell the truth
Of everything he'd seen,
But Fang was still determined
That he would vent his spleen.

For Mr Brownlow had remarked,
'I browsed books at a stall'
When he was stopped unpleasantly.
He said no more at all;

For Fang told him to hold his tongue
And to the policeman said,
'Are there no witnesses to hear?'
The policeman shook his head.

'No your worship, none at all.'
Fang, in his irate fashion
Turned to Brownlow and he said,
In a towering passion,

'Don't just stand there, state your case.'
He spoke with angry scorn.
'What's your complaint against the boy?
Speak up, for you've been sworn.

'And now if you refuse to speak
And do not show respect,
I promise you it will not pass
Without sir, being checked.

'For I will punish you, so speak
And tell us what you saw.'
So harassed Mr Brownlow – now
Tried to speak once more.

He did his best to then explain
That the tumultuous fray,
Had only chased poor Oliver
Because he'd run away.

He said, 'The boy's been hurt enough.
Be lenient on him.'
'Oh yes, I dare say,' Fang replied,
With tone both terse and grim.

At this point Oliver then asked
'Could I have some water?'
'Stuff and nonsense,' Fang replied,
Giving him no quarter.

Then Oliver fell over.
He fainted on the floor.
The officer jumped forward,
For he felt some rapport…

With the poor, unhappy lad
And he could clearly see
That Oliver was really sick,
But Fang yelled, 'Let him be.

'He can lie there on the floor.
It's nothing but flimflam.
I've seen this kind of thing before.
It's just a silly sham.'

The Clerk then asked the awful Fang,
'How do you propose
To deal with this dishonest lad?'
The foul man stroked his nose.

'He stands committed for three months,'
Fang declared with force,
And then he added savagely,
'Hard labour too, of course.'

Two stalwart men stepped forward
Now ready to convey
Poor Oliver to prison –
To take the lad away.

But as they did, a man appeared,
In quite a breathless state.
He cried out loudly, 'Stop, please stop.
For heaven's sake – please wait.'

'What's this?' Fang cried. 'Get out of here.'
The man began to shout.
'I will not go, I will be heard.
For I'll not be turned out.

'I saw it happen – everything,
So you must hear it all.
I will be sworn, for Mr Fang –
I run the small bookstall.'

'Well, swear the fellow in,' Fang said
With stony, angry face,
And with a manner showing
Distaste and such ill grace.

'Now then – what have you got to say?'
The man spoke loud and clear.
'You've apprehended in this court
The wrong young lad, I fear.

'I saw the theft. 'Twas not this boy.
It was another one.
This lad looked on quite stupefied
At what was being done.'

'Why didn't you come here before?'
Said Fang in angry tone.
'I had no-one to mind the stall.
I was there on my own.'

Fang turned to Mr Brownlow then.
He said, 'So what's your ploy,
That you prefer a charge against
An innocent, poor boy?

'Now let this be a lesson for
You'll find that you will get,
Into trouble with the law –
'Twill overtake you yet.'

Mr Brownlow burst with rage
At all that had occurred.
Then 'Clear the office – do you hear.'
Was all the poor man heard.

He had no chance to remonstrate
For all reply was barred,
And so he was conveyed with force
Out into the yard.

And there he saw poor Oliver –
His anger disappeared.
The boy was white and trembling
And Mr Brownlow feared…

That he was very ill indeed,
For he made not a sound.
A sad and sorry bundle as
He lay there on the ground.

Mr Brownlow cried, 'Poor boy.
Oh fetch a coach I pray.'
And then with care he bore the lad
Most speedily away.

The bookstall owner went with them –
And driving down a mews,
These gentlemen there both agreed,
There was no time to lose.

OLIVER FALLS INTO KINDLY HANDS

The coach rattled down Mount Pleasant,
And past the Angel too,
Then to Pentonville to where
A neat house came in view.

They carried Oliver inside
And gently placed him in
A snug, inviting bed which had
Soft blankets to his chin.

And there he lay for many days –
A fever gripped the lad.
He lay there thin and deathly pale;
A scene so awfully sad.

But then one day he raised himself
Feebly on one arm.
'What room is this?' His quaking voice
Was filled with mild alarm.

'Hush, hush, my dear,' a lady said,
As softly she drew near.
'You must lie quiet for you've been
Very ill I fear.

'So lie down now and rest some more.'
She said this with such care,
As gently then she laid him back
And smoothed his flowing hair.

She did it with such kindliness,
In such a loving way;
All her caring qualities
Were clearly on display.

Oliver placed his withered hand
Upon the lady's there,
Then drew it round his wasted neck
With such a grateful air.

The worried lady sighed aloud
And said, 'Oh, what a dear.
What would his darling mother feel
If she was with him here.'

'Perhaps she has sat with us ma'am,'
The boy sighed languidly.
He placed his hands as if in prayer.
'Perhaps she does see me.'

He fell into a gentle doze.
He lay there weak and wan.
And as he slept, but fitfully
The night crept slowly on.

Three days passed – the doctor said,
Having thought at length,
That Oliver could now get up
For he had gained some strength.

They propped him in an easy chair.
The lady sat with him.
Her name was Mrs Bedwin and
Her eyes began to brim.

For tears welled up within them both,
They ran down both her cheeks,
And left her face quite covered in
Long, shiny silver streaks.

Her tears were caused by sheer delight,
To see him sitting there.
She knew he must be getting well
By taking to the chair.

'Never mind, my dear,' she said,
Heaving a deep sigh,
'It does me good in having just
A regular good cry.

'It's over now – I'm comfortable.'
Her manner seemed more calm.
Oliver looked across and said,
'You're kind to me, dear ma'am.'

Later on the lady saw
Oliver in thrall
With a lovely portrait that
Was hanging on the wall.

'Are you fond of pictures dear?'
She asked in kindly way.
'I've seen so few,' the boy replied,
'And so it's hard to say,

'But that lady in the picture
Has such a lovely face.'
His carer smiled and readily
Agreed this was the case.

Mr Brownlow now appeared,
He looked down on the lad;
His face went through contortions –
But mostly he seemed glad,

For though the boy looked sickly,
He felt that he could tell,
Despite his worn out countenance,
That he was getting well.

Oliver then –for his part –
Raised his withered hand,
Then from respect, and nothing more
Made an attempt to stand.

The effort was too much – he sank
Back in the chair again,
And Mr Brownlow's tears then fell
Like gentle drops of rain,

For in his breast he had a heart
Large enough to serve
At least six kindly gentlemen
With some still in reserve.

'Poor boy, poor boy,' he whispered
And then more of the same.
He gave him ample sympathy
And then he asked his name.

Oliver gave it honestly
And as he softly spoke,
Mr Brownlow looked around
And spied there in a stroke…

The portrait on the wall and saw –
As he looked at the boy –
They were the same, could this just be
Some new, imagined ploy?

But no – the eyes, the head, the mouth
Did massively proclaim
That they were copies, so alike,
Each feature just the same.

Mr Brownlow cried aloud
But knew not what to say,
And Oliver, still awfully weak
Just fainted clean away.

BILL SIKES

Now Charley Bates and Dodger
Had made their getaway.
It was no time to hang around.
But what would Fagin say?

They ran and ran until quite puffed,
And when they took a rest,
Charley Bates began to laugh;
He thought it all a jest.

'What's so funny?' Dodger asked.
And then he lost his cool.
'Hold your noise or folk will look.
Don't be a silly fool.'

But still young Charley laughed and laughed.
'Can't help it,' he cried out.
'To see him running at that pace
And dodging all about,

'And cutting round those corners
And chasing up a lane,
And knocking into posts and then
Just starting off again.

'And me there with the 'andkerchief
Safely in my pocket,
And singing after him while he
Takes off like a rocket.

'Oh 'pon my eye, I never saw
On any night or day,
A funnier thing.' Then Dodger said,
'But what will Fagin say?'

Charley just replied with 'What?'
And Dodger said no more.
He merely pulled a face for now
They were at Fagin's door.

Fagin heard them as they climbed
The creaking, groaning stairs;
He roused himself from working at
His menial affairs.

He turned around, his pale white face
Held a rascally smile,
But then he changed, his face now held
A look of bile and guile.

'Why, how's this, there's only two.
Whatever has occurred?'
He listened to their footsteps.
'What's happened to the third?'

The footsteps now approached and then
Through the door they came,
Charley Bates and Dodger,
Oh yes – the very same,

But not a sign of Oliver,
And Fagin then cried out,
'Where's the boy?' His anger rose.
'So what's this all about?

'What's been goin' on, you hounds?'
His face a crimson hue.
He grabbed the Dodger and cried 'Speak.
Or I will throttle you.

'Will you speak?' he thundered out.
My word he did look grim.
Dodger sullenly confessed,
'The traps have taken him.'

The Dodger broke away and then
He grabbed the toasting fork
And took a lunge at Fagin who
Moved swiftly – like a hawk –

And grabbed a pot of beer intent
To throw it at the Dodger.
His speed defied the notion that
He was a bent, old codger.

But as he went to throw it
Charley cried out loud,
So Fagin aimed the pot at him,
But then a voice avowed…

'I'll settle with the hand that pitched
That pot of beer at me.
It's just as well 'twas only beer
That hit me or you'd see…

'I would have settled somebody –
But wouldn't you just know,
That only stupid Fagin
Would be inclined to throw…

'Good beer around as if it was
Just water – what a mess.
So Fagin – what's it all about?
Come on – don't make me guess.'

The man who growled these words with ire
Was rough and mean of face,
With bulky legs, he was quite stout
And now he filled the space…

At the door – he'd just come in
And his enormous size,
Combined with three days growth of beard
And two, sharp, scowling eyes,

And top hat and black overcoat
And dirty, greasy look,
Created then as drab a rogue
As any from a book.

And then he turned around and growled,
'Come in. Come in, d'ye hear.'
A shaggy, white dishevelled dog,
That followed at the rear…

Came skulking in and looked about
As fearful dogs will do.
'Why didn't you come in before?
Whatever's wrong with you?'

The man was angry and annoyed,
His face an awful frown.
'Are you too proud to be with me?
Get over there – lie down.'

He gave the dog a hefty kick.
The dog, without a sound,
Ran to a corner of the room
And lay upon the ground.

He seemed well used to ill abuse.
He curled up in a ball,
As if to do his very best
To make himself look small.

Then the man spoke out again.
'Fagin, wot yer doin?
You ill-treatin' boys again?
Some day 'twill be yer ruin.

'I wonder they don't murder you.
If I'd bin in their gang
I'd have done it years ago
Or somehow seen yer hang.'

'Hush, Mr Sikes,' old Fagin said.
'My dear, don't speak so loud.'
'You're up to mischief ain't yer,'
The ruffian then avowed.

'For when yer start a-mistering,
Well mischief's in yer sight.
So don't come that old game with me.
Yer know my name all right.'

Fagin said, 'Well, well, Bill Sikes,
Now are you feeling ill?
You're not yourself, you seem to be
Quite out of humour Bill.'

Sikes ignored the comment then
Demanded liquor 'Now!
And mind that you don't poison it.'
Old Fagin made a bow…

And turning to a cupboard
He gave an evil leer,
As if to indicate he'd love
To make Bill Sikes feel queer.

When Sikes had downed a glass or two
The conversation turned,
To Oliver and everything
The Dodger had discerned.

Finally old Fagin said,
'I am inclined to think
He'll get us all in trouble
And see us all in clink,

Or even worse.' He shivered then,
And also softly swore,
That if the game is up for us –
Could be for many more.

Then turning to Bill Sikes he said,
'Yes Bill, I truly fear
That it could be much worse for you
Than all of us, my dear.'

Sikes then started with a jolt
As Fagin looked away.
A silence fell for nobody
Knew now what to say.

At last Bill Sikes spoke up – he said,
'Somebody must find out
What's bin 'appening – someone
Must go and 'ave a scout.'

Fagin nodded – Bill then said,
'If that kid hasn't peached,
We must ensure before he does
The little devil's reached.

'When he comes out he must be grabbed
And taken care of too.'
Old Fagin nodded knowing
'Twas what they'd have to do.

The only problem then of course
Was choosing who should go,
For everybody present saw
The law as their main foe.

So going to their office
For anything – whatever –
Was something that they wouldn't do
Today – tomorrow – never!

No, Charley Bates nor Dodger
Or any of their likes,
Or Fagin or especially
Violent Bill Sikes…

Would ever go to such a place,
Not in a hundred years,
It represented everything
That summed up all their fears.

They sat and pondered long and hard
'Bout dealing with the law,
When a solution entered then
Through Fagin's battered door.

'Twas Bet and Nancy who came in.
Fagin cried with glee.
'Bet, my dear, come over here
And have a word with me.'

But when she heard what he proposed
She said quite clearly 'No!'
It was the last place in the world
That she would choose to go.

So Fagin turned to Nancy.
He softly called her name.
'What do you say? Now will you go?'
Her answer was the same.

'Oh, she will go all right,' said Bill.
Nancy bawled, 'I won't.'
'She does what she is told,' he yelled.
And Nancy cried, 'I don't.'

But Sikes was right as always,
For threats – they did the trick;
So Nancy set off then to seek
Oliver – at the Nick.

Before she went she played a joke
By bursting into tears,
And cried, 'My little brother,
For now my worst held fears…

'Have come to pass – I've lost him.
Oh gentlemen, I pray,
Please have you seen a little boy
Just roaming round today?'

Nancy smiled and they all laughed.
She cried, 'I'm so afeared.'
She paused before the company,
Then winked and disappeared.

Fagin turned to his young friends
To recognise their cheers.
He shook his head and gravely said,
'A clever girl, my dears.'

And Sikes filled up his glass and drank
With one flick of his wrist,
And then he banged the table hard
With his almighty fist.

'She's a 'onour to 'er sex, she is,'
He said with drunken slur.
'Here's to 'er 'ealth – I surely wish
All women were like 'er.'

NANCY MAKES SOME ENQUIRIES

Nancy made her anxious way
And with a little fear,
Through the tangled streets and to
The grim police station's rear.

She entered by the old back door.
There was no sound within.
And now began the great pretence
Of looking for her kin.

She looked upon the strong cell doors
And then she made her choice,
And knocked on one and gently said,
In nervous, quaking voice,

'Nolly dear, are you there?'
But cowering inside
Was a shoeless criminal
Who shook and cried and sighed.

Nancy moved along and knocked
Upon another cell,
And from inside she heard a noise.
A feeble voice cried 'Well?'

'Is there a little boy in there?'
Asked Nancy with a sob.
'No, God forbid,' came the reply
From some downtrodden slob.

The next cell was the same as well.
Just one more abject soul,
Incarcerated in that foul,
Unpleasant, dismal hole.

So Nancy made her way towards
The officer in charge.
He wore a bright striped waistcoat which
Was really very large.

It covered his huge stomach.
Nancy wailed, and thus
With fervent lamentations
Created quite a fuss.

She cried out, 'Where's my brother?
Where is the little dear?'
The officer replied and said,
'I haven't got him here.'

'Where is he then?' screamed Nancy.
The officer just sighed.
'The gentleman has got him,'
He carelessly replied.

'What gentleman?' asked Nancy.
'Gracious heavens above.
Who is this gentleman – please tell –
Who's got my little love?'

The officer explained it all
And said the boy was ill.
'And so he's now been taken to
A house in Pentonville.'

Nancy staggered out the door
As if she was undone,
But once she turned the corner
She broke into a run.

She went straight back to Fagin's place
And there they all agreed,
There was just one thing they must do –
Oh yes, a pressing need.

To find young Oliver and then
Kidnap him right away.
It must be done and rapidly –
They couldn't risk delay.

Fagin said, 'He must be found.
You boys must find just where
Oliver is being held
And get him out of there.

'It seems he hasn't peached so far,
So all of you now GET.
For if he means to blab we may
Just stop his windpipe yet!'

OLIVER RUNS AN ERRAND FOR MR BROWNLOW

Over the ensuing weeks
We can now gladly tell,
That Oliver grew stronger and
Began to feel quite well.

And so he made his way downstairs
Upon a sunny day,
And noticed that the picture
Had now been put away.

The one that looked so very much
Like Oliver himself.
He searched around the walls and looked
At every nook and shelf.

Mrs Bedwin said, 'It's gone,
For Mr Brownlow thought
It worried you and was convinced
It made you feel distraught.'

'Oh no,' cried Oliver, dismayed,
'I loved to see it there,
And now it's gone the vacant wall
Looks dismal and quite bare.'

'So you get well,' the lady said,
'And then I'm sure once more
We'll hang the picture up again
Just where it was before.'

And so the days passed pleasantly
And Oliver held dear,
The fact that he no longer
Had any cause to fear.

And then one day, the happy boy
Tapped on the study door
Where Mr Brownlow sat alone,
And Oliver then saw…

The gentleman was reading,
Sitting in his chair,
And there were books aplenty
Around him, everywhere.

Oliver was astounded
To see so many books.
Mr Brownlow saw at once
His open-mouthed, rapt looks.

'There are a lot of them,' he said
'Some fat, some thin, some small.
If you are good, behave yourself,
Why, you shall read them all.'

Then Mr Brownlow's manner changed,
Becoming now quite serious;
But kindly though and not at all
Scary or imperious.

'I want to have a little talk
Now you seem well today.'
Poor Oliver was quite alarmed,
'Oh, don't send me away!

'Oh let me be a servant,
Or anything you name.
Don't send me to that wretched place
From which, kind sir, I came.'

Mr Brownlow was surprised.
The outburst made him pause.
He said, 'I won't desert you lad,
Unless you give me cause.'

'I never will,' vowed Oliver.
The old man sat quite still.
He said, 'I really hope you won't,
And I don't think you will,

'For in the past I've been deceived
By others that I knew,
But I feel strongly that I can
Put all my trust in you.

'And though the people that I've loved
The most in all the world,'
(And here his deepest, heartfelt thoughts
He quietly unfurled)

'Now lie within their graves and so
We have been cast apart,
I haven't sealed myself and made
A coffin of my heart.

'For I believe affliction
Sometimes will unfetter
Goodwill towards our fellow man
And make our nature better.

'I tell you this so you're aware
That I have felt great pain,
So you'll perhaps be careful
To spare me that again.

'Now let me hear your story.
Tell it and take your time,
And if I find you're innocent
Of doing any crime...

'You'll find I will be generous
In everything I give.
You'll never be without a friend
For all the time I live.'

Oliver sobbed a little
Then raised his trembling chin,
Wiped his eyes and coughed and made
Quite ready to begin.

But then they heard a knocking on
The house's large front door,
And then a servant's feet were heard
A-clicking on the floor.

And then the servant entered,
And said, 'I've come to say
Your good friend Mr Grimwig
Has called on you today.

'He asked if there was any chance
His dear, best friend was free,
And also was it possible
That muffins were for tea?'

Mr Brownlow smiled and said
'Show him in right away.'
Oliver asked if he should go.
The old man said, 'No, stay.'

And then a moment later –
Walked Grimwig through the door,
Marked by the great blue overcoat
And wide brimmed hat he wore.

He had a bright, striped waistcoat
And carried a large stick
Which helped him walk, it really was
Extremely strong and thick.

He leant on it with his full weight,
Then struck it on the mat,
Then looked across at Oliver
And said, 'Hallo! What's that?'

Mr Brownlow carefully
Gripped Oliver's small wrist
And pulled him forward saying,
'Why this is Master Twist.

'The little boy we spoke about.'
'That's him?' Grimwig replied.
'Yes, that's the boy, the very one,'
Said Brownlow as he sighed.

'How are you boy?' asked Grimwig.
His manner was most blunt.
'Much better now,' said Oliver.
From Grimwig – just a grunt.

But Mr Brownlow smiled and said –
Ignoring Grimwig's stares –
'Oliver – now will you please
Go and step downstairs,

'And see if tea is ready.'
Oliver left the pair.
'Nice looking boy,' said Brownlow,
And Grimwig sitting there…

Said gloomily and pettishly,
'I really do not know,
For I see just two kinds of boys
As round this world I go.

'There's mealy boys and beef-faced boys.'
Good Mr Brownlow sighed,
And said, 'So which is Oliver?'
'Mealy,' Grimwig cried.

And thus they chatted on through tea
With Mr Brownlow being
Supportive of young Oliver,
But Grimwig only seeing…

Bad things in the boy – their views
Were strong and running rife,
Till Brownlow said, 'I'll back that boy
And do it with my life.'

Mr Grimwig looked at him
And very brusquely said,
'And I'll avow his falsehood
And answer with my head.'

'Well we shall see,' said Brownlow
And with a rising passion.
'We will indeed,' said Grimwig
In his annoying fashion.

The men stared at each other
With angry, rigid looks,
Then Mrs Bedwin entered.
She held a pack of books.

'These have been delivered.
A boy just brought them here.'
'Oh, stop him,' Mr Brownlow said.
The lady cried, 'I fear…

That he has left already.'
He said, 'I've got a pack
Of books that I've rejected
And should be taken back.

'I also owe the bookseller
Some money – it's not right
That he should not be paid at once.
I want it done tonight.'

'Send Oliver,' said Grimwig.
'Yes, let the fellow go.
He'll get the books there safely.
I'm sure he will, you know.'

Mr Brownlow thought at first
That he would not agree,
But knew his friend was baiting him
And so he thought he'd see…

What would happen if the boy
Was sent off on this task,
For he was certain he'd return.
Was it too much to ask?

Oliver was keen to go –
To take the books and pay.
He said, 'Oh, let me take them,
And I'll run all the way.'

He put his cap upon his head.
Pulled on his little coat.
Then Mr Brownlow handed him
A crispy, five pound note.

'Now tell the bookstall owner
That you have come to pay
The money that I owe to him,
And you must also say…

'You've brought this little pile of books,
For they are not required.'
Oliver replied and said
He'd do as he desired.

'I'll be back in ten minutes sir.'
He headed for the door.
Mrs Bedwin saw him out
But on her face she wore…

A very worried look as she
Sent him into the night.
'I cannot bear to let him go
Or let him from my sight.'

She smiled then as she waved to him.
'Oh, bless his little face.'
And Oliver took off as if
He ran in some great race.

The gentlemen now settled down,
Eager then to learn
What would happen – would the boy
Run off, or soon return?

Mr Brownlow took his watch
And placed it on the table.
He said, 'I think that Oliver
Will easily be able…

'To get back here quite quickly,
In fact I am quite sure
He will be back and safely
In half an hour – no more.'

Mr Grimwig frowned at him.
His face looked set and black.
'And so you really do expect
The fellow will come back?'

'Don't you?' came Brownlow's curt riposte.
'I don't,' Grimwig replied.
'For when he said he'd be right back
I somehow felt he lied.

'He's got new clothing on his back,
And five pounds in his hand.
Expensive books to sell – my friend
You surely understand…

'He'll join his thieving friends and laugh,
For he's a sneaky brat.
I tell you now, if he returns
I'll surely eat my hat.'

And thus they sat in silence.
It grew pitch black outside,
And still they sat and both of them
Were motionless and eyed…

The ticking watch, but very soon
The dial was hard to see,
And Mr Brownlow wondered then –
Where could the young lad be?

OLIVER IS KIDNAPPED

And so young Oliver ran on
Going at pell-mell.
He made his way through ill-lit streets
And then in Clerkenwell…

He heard a woman screaming,
She called out in a stew,
'Oh, here's my darling brother.
Oh yes, it's really you.'

He stopped to have a look and see
What it was all about,
And as he did the woman gave
Another piercing shout.

And then she threw her chubby arms
Around his neck and cried,
'Where have you been? Why did you go
And run away and hide?'

'Leave me alone,' cried Oliver.
'Let go of me right now.'
But all he heard was wailing.
My word she made a row.

'Oh my gracious, deary me,
I've found him now at last.
Oh Oliver – oh Oliver.
We've all been so downcast.

'You naughty boy – where have you been?
You've caused us such distress.
Whatever you've been doing
I can but only guess.'

With further exclamations,
So loud and high and shrill,
She carried on hysterically
And didn't cease until…

Two women came upon the scene
And said, 'Are you all right?'
'Oh yes,' she said, 'I'm really fine
Now that I've found this mite.

'He's caused such consternation.
He's my naughty brother.
He's caused such worry and distress
To me and to our mother.

'He ran away a month ago.
The little, mean upstart.
He joined a gang of thieving rogues
And broke his mother's heart.'

'You little wretch,' a woman yelled.
Her voice was also shrill.
'I'm not a wretch,' cried Oliver.
'I live in Pentonville.

'She's not my sister and I'm not
A thief or mean and bad.
I don't know who she is and I
Don't have a mum or dad.

'I'm an orphan – leave me be.'
And then he looked around.
'Why it's Nancy,' he exclaimed.
She made a sighing sound.

'You see he knows me,' she cried out.
'And now I'm sure you'll see
What a selfish boy he is.
He'll be the death of me.'

And then a man came bursting out
From a dim beer shop,
And seeing him made Nancy then
Very quickly stop.

She ceased her wailing and her noise
For standing there she saw
Grim Bill Sikes, his dog as well,
And Bill then loudly swore,

'What the devil's all this then?
I'll teach yer lad to roam.
Yer coming back to mother now.
I'm taking you back home.'

Oliver cried out lustily.
'Help me. Help me please.
I don't belong with them – I don't.
I'm begging on my knees.'

'Help!' cried Sikes. 'I'll give yer help.
Yer little rascal you.
If yer don't behave yerself,
Yer know what I will do?

'But what are these? What are these books?
Yer been a-stealing lad?
Give 'em 'ere yer wicked rogue.
I'll stop yer acting bad.'

And so he grabbed the pack of books
And struck a heavy blow
Across poor Oliver's small head.
He cried, 'That's so yer know…

'Don't mess with me yer villain –
I'll tear yer limb from limb.'
Then turning to his dog he said,
'Bullseye – keep watch on 'im'

Oliver was terrified
And dizzy from the blows,
And frightened by this fierce attack
And still too in the throes…

Of getting over being ill,
And scared to bits and by
The growling of the awful dog
That viewed him with one eye.

And overpowered, for he knew
The people looking on
Thought he was just a naughty boy
And guilty of a con.

What could he do? Why nothing,
For darkness had set in,
And he was being dragged with force
Which made his poor head spin.

Through narrow courts and alley ways,
On and on they ran,
And all the time poor Oliver
Was held by that foul man.

And no-one took much notice.
Nobody seemed to care,
That such a little boy was in
Such awful trouble there.

~ ~ ~

The gas lamps were now lighted.
The servants checked the street,
Hoping they'd find Oliver
Not guilty of deceit.

They prayed they'd see him coming,
Running down the road,
Eager now to get back to
His happy new abode.

And Mrs Bedwin waited
At the open door
Thinking, 'Here comes Oliver.'
But 'twasn't what she saw.

It was but an illusion.
There really was no trace
Of little Oliver's frail form
And his pale, smiling face.

And still the two, old gentlemen
Sat each upon a chair –
In the dark and motionless,
The watch just ticking there.

WHAT BECAME OF OLIVER

'Take Nancy's hand,' Bill Sikes declared.
Oliver quaked with fear.
'Take 'er 'and I say – and mine.
Do it now d'ya 'ear.

'And Bullseye, if 'e speaks a word,
Yer know just what to do.
D'ya 'ear that boy, Bullseye 'ere
Can sort the likes of you.'

And so they walked in pouring rain
Down dirty, narrow ways,
And Oliver trudged on – his mind
Just one lost, jumbled haze.

Then finally they reached a door
Along a darkened street.
Not the sort of place you'd find
That decent folk would meet.

The door was softly opened,
They all three stepped inside,
Then someone chained and barred the door.
Sikes said –all evil eyed…

'Is the old 'un 'ere tonight?'
'Oh yes,' a voice came back.
'And precious down of mouth 'e is.
'Is mood's been really black.'

Oliver recognised the voice,
And when a light was lit
He saw the Dodger standing there,
And he saw humour flit…

Across the Dodger's face and then
He bade them follow him,
And once again he found himself
In that room dank and grim.

When Charley Bates espied him
He cried, 'My wig. My wig.'
He called out then to Fagin
And did a little jig.

'Fagin, look at 'im,' he cried.
'Oh, hold me while I laugh.
Look at his togs there Fagin.
Oh what a lovely scarf.

'And see this fancy jacket,
The cloth is superfine.
So where you orf to Oliver?
Yer goin' out ter dine?'

Now Fagin bowed down very low
With mock humility.
'How nice of you to come, my dear.
It is so good to see…

'You're looking well.' Then Charley Bates
Let out a raucous hoot.
And Fagin said, 'The Dodger here
Will put away your suit.

'You mustn't spoil your Sunday best,
So we'll take care of that.
We'll find another coat and all
And even a top hat.

'So take a seat right here my dear.
Would you like a cuppa?
We didn't know you planned to come.
Will you stay for supper?'

As he spoke he then removed
Oliver's smart coat.
'You should have written to us dear.
Sent us a little note,

'And told us you were coming round –
For we'd have got things ready.'
Charley Bates laughed out so much
His legs went all unsteady.

Then Dodger placed his probing hand
In Oliver's fine coat
And in an instant he drew out
The crispy five pound note.

Fagin grabbed the note straight off.
Bill Sikes cried, 'Oy, that's mine.'
Fagin raised his hand and spoke,
His voice a crafty whine.

'No, no, my dear. It shall be mine.'
They exchanged fierce looks.
'No, I shall keep the five pound note
And you shall have the books.'

'If that ain't mine,' Bill Sikes replied,
His eyes flashed wild and black.
'Well mine and Nancy's too of course –
I'll take the boy right back.'

'This isn't fair,' old Fagin snarled.
Sikes yelled, 'Well fair or not,
You'll hand it over right away
You crafty old despot.

'Do you think Nancy 'ere and me
Got nothing else to do,
Than wasting precious time to go
A-grabbing kids for you?

'You avaricious skeleton.
I'll tell yer, I ain't pleading.
You can have the books to keep,
That's if yer fond of reading.

'If not – well sell 'em.' Fagin then
Just stared back looking glum.
He held the five pound note between
His finger and his thumb.

In one swift move Sikes plucked it out,
Then folded it quite small,
And smirked in pleasure at this fine
And unexpected haul.

And Charley Bates then grabbed a book
And with a little sneer,
Pretended that he read and vowed,
'Lovely writing 'ere.'

Oliver fell onto his knees,
'Oh send them back I pray.
They're owned by an old gentleman,
I'd hate for him to say…

'I stole them and so I'm a thief.
Please send them back tonight.'
Fagin rubbed his hands and cried,
'Of course, the boy is right.

'They'll think he stole them – what a joke,
It's worked out very well.'
Oliver listened carefully
To see if he could tell…

Just what old Fagin meant by this.
Then he could stand no more
And jumping to his feet he rushed
Towards the run-down door.

He yelled for help and Nancy cried,
'Hold Bullseye back there Bill.
He'll tear the boy to pieces.
He'll go in for the kill.'

'It serves him right,' cried Sikes with glee.
'Get orf me right away.
I'll split yer skull upon the wall.
Stand off from me, I say.'

'I won't,' she screamed. 'I tell you Bill
You can just do your worst.
The child shall not be torn apart
Unless you kill me first.'

Bill Sikes then flung the girl aside
And left off his attack,
For Fagin and two boys had now
Dragged Oliver right back.

'You wished to get away my dear?'
Said Fagin angrily.
'Going off to get the police.
Well, I'll cure that, you'll see.'

He grabbed a jagged club that lay
By the old fireplace.
A horrid, mean and awful look
Invaded his old face.

And then he struck small Oliver
A heavy, vicious blow,
And raised it for a second time,
But Nancy cried out, 'No!'

She wrestled it from out his hand
And threw it in the fire.
'I won't stand by and see it done –
What more do you require?

'You've got the boy, so let him be
Or I'll commit a crime –
To take me to the gallows
A bit before my time.'

'Nancy dear,' old Fagin said.
His tone was soft and light,
'You're acting very clever
And beautifully tonight.'

'Am I?' she cried angrily,
'Don't push it, let it be,
Or you will be the worst for it
So keep well clear of me.'

There's something 'bout a woman
When she is in a rage
That makes most men decide they won't
Oppose them or engage.

So Fagin shrank back awkwardly
But Sikes said with a growl,
As if addressing Bullseye,
And in a tone quite foul…

And in a manner that implied
It was quite understood
He'd be obeyed – 'Keep quiet or
I'll quiet yer for good.'

Nancy laughed and nervously
But not a word was said.
She looked at Sikes then bit her lip
So hard until it bled.

'You're a nice 'un ain't yer,'
Bill Sikes's eyes looked wild.
'To act humane and so genteel
And for this worthless child.'

'God almighty, so I am,'
The girl said with a sneer.
'I wish I'd been struck dead, I do
Before I brought him here.

'For he's a thief, a liar now.
A devil? Heaven knows.
So surely that's enough without
That mean, old wretch's blows.'

'Come, come, my dear,' old Fagin cried.
His manner was appealing.
'We must have civil words – we must.'
Nancy cried with feeling...

'Civil words! Civil words!'
My she was in a passion.
'Civil words you villain you.'
Her face had turned quite ashen.

'Yes you deserve such words from me.'
Fagin's face looked grim.
'For I was thieving for you when
But half as old as him.'

She pointed to young Oliver
And Fagin rubbed his chin.
'It was your living dear,' he said.
'So that can't be a sin.'

'My living is it?' screamed the girl.
'Out on the dirty street,
That's been my home, out in the wet,
The fog, the snow, the sleet.

'And you're the wretch that drove me there.'
She gave a woeful cry.
'And likely that is where I'll be
Until the day I die.'

She rushed at Fagin angrily
Intent to make him pay.
And she'd have left her mark on him
But Sikes stood in her way.

She struggled for a moment
And then without a sound,
She went quite limp and lifelessly
She fainted on the ground.

'She's all right now,' Bill Sikes declared.
Fagin said, 'That's fine,
For women are essential in
Our very special line.'

Then Charley Bates piped up and asked
With tone of implied sorrow,
'Should Oliver wear his brand new togs
When he gets up tomorrow?'

'Certainly not,' old Fagin smiled.
And Charley laughed out loud.
'It wouldn't do if Oliver
Stood out when in a crowd.'

And as for Oliver – well he
Didn't make a peep.
He was so sick and weary that
He soon fell fast asleep.

A ROBBERY IS PLANNED

Oliver was now confined
To Fagin's cheerless room.
All he knew o'er coming days
Was its dark, dismal gloom.

And he was at the mercy
Of Fagin's changing mood,
He thought that keeping Oliver
In gloom and solitude…

Would make the boy just grateful
For any company,
And Fagin felt quite certain that
All in good time he'd see…

Oliver come round and then –
Just to gain relief –
Would finally and happily
Become a full-time thief.

Oh yes, that evil Fagin
Had now made it his goal
To drop a dose of poison
Into the poor boy's soul.

But then one damp and chilly night
When that old north wind blew,
Fagin said he must go out
For he had work to do.

He buttoned up his tatty coat
Around his shrivelled form,
Then pulled the collar round his ears
To fend off any storm,

Then stepping out into the street
He turned to make quite sure
That the boys inside had now
Securely locked the door.

And then he slunk off down the street
All bent and thin and old.
A dirty mist hung all about;
The air was clammy cold.

It seemed as if the dismal night
Depressingly assured
A scene befitting perfectly
For him to be abroad.

He glided stealthily along,
Quite hideous and vile.
In many ways he seemed just like
A loathsome, dark reptile.

He kept on course through alleyways
As grim as any seen,
All winding, narrow, miserable,
Till he reached Bethnal Green.

And then he turned into a lane
Lit by a single light,
And rapped upon a scruffy door,
Then waited in the night.

A dog growled then a voice was heard.
It yelled, 'What's that I hear?'
'It's only me Bill,' Fagin said.
'It's only me, my dear.'

'Well bring yer body in,' Sikes yelled.
'Don't stand around out there.'
So Fagin shuffled through the door,
Then plonked down in a chair.

Sikes sat before the meagre fire.
With Nancy there as well,
Intent upon a quiet night
As far as one could tell.

Nancy said, 'It's very cold.'
Fagin said he knew.
He warmed his hands above the fire,
And said, 'It chills right through.'

Sikes said, 'It must be very cold
To reach your wicked 'eart.
Give 'im a drink for mercy's sake
Afore we make a start,

'For it could make a man quite ill
To see that lean, old knave,
A-shivering like an ugly ghost
Just rose from out the grave.'

Nancy fetched some brandy
And bade cold Fagin drink.
He took a swig and then he said,
'That's quite enough I think.

'I don't indulge a lot, my dear.
I'm happy with just one.
So now then Bill, the Chertsey job.
When is it to be done?'

Sikes scratched his head and thus replied,
With darting, evil eyes,
'As soon as I can find myself
A lad the proper size.

'I need a thin and little lad
To help to steal the gear.'
'Use Oliver,' cried Fagin then.
'He's the boy, my dear.

'He's been in training now for weeks.'
Bill Sikes just took a swig.
He thought a bit as Fagin said,
'The others are too big.'

'Well he's the size all right,' said Sikes,
'Of that I am quite sure.'
And Nancy said, 'All he must do
Is open up a door.'

'He'll do exactly what you want.'
Old Fagin's tone was rough.
'Just make quite certain Bill, my dear
You scare the boy enough.'

'Scare him Fagin,' Sikes replied.
'If he should choose to shirk,
Or act in any way that's queer
Once we are 'ard at work…

'Well if he does, I can 'ere say
The boy will not survive.
I promise Fagin, ne'er again
Will you see him alive.

'So think on that afore yer send
The boy to work with me.'
He pulled a crowbar from the floor
For Fagin there to see.

'For if he let's me down,' he cried,
'I'll smash this 'cross his 'ead.'
'Don't worry for I've thought it through,'
The awful Fagin said.

'I've come to the conclusion
And it is my belief,
That once I've made young Oliver
Convinced he is a thief…

'Why then he will be ours for life,
We'll own that wretched boy.'
Then at this point he hugged himself
Quite literally with joy.

'Ours,' cried Sikes. 'He's yours you mean,
To do just as you bid.
But why take all this trouble
For one chalk-faced, young kid?

'There's fifty of them every night
A-snoozing in the street,
And every one would be prepared
To lie and steal and cheat.'

Fagin said, 'I tell you Bill
They're just no use to me,
For if they get in trouble,
Well anyone can see…

'The way they look convicts them –
Condemns them to disgrace.
But Oliver looks innocent
Because of his sweet face.

'Right now the boy could finger us
By opening his gob,
But he'll be guilty like us all
Once he has done a job.

'For I'll have power over him.
He never will break free.
For he'll be like the rest of us –
Oh yes – a thief he'll be.

'And what's to lose for I believe
That you would likely say
It's better than we put the boy
Completely out the way.'

Sikes nodded and then Fagin said,
His argument now won,
'So tell me Bill, this robbery.
When is it to be done?'

Sikes scratched his head and then replied
'I planned to do it soon
The night arter tomorrow –
When there is little moon.

'So bring the boy on over.'
Nancy said, 'But better still
I'll come and get him Fagin –
And bring him here to Bill.'

And so it was agreed and thus
Dark Fagin left the place.
He made his way from whence he'd come,
A smile upon his face.

He dodged his way through mud and mire,
Along the grimy road,
Till finally and gratefully
He reached his mean abode.

The Dodger there was waiting
And wily Fagin said,
'I want to speak to Oliver.
Now is the lad abed?'

'Hours ago,' said Dodger.
'He's sleeping over there.'
Fagin went to where he lay
And looked with stony stare.

The boy was lying still, he seemed
To hardly draw a breath,
So sad and pale and anxious
That he looked just like death.

Not death as seen within a shroud,
So cold and broken hearted,
But in the guise that's worn by death
When life has just departed.

In that soft instant when the soul
Has left the world's gross air
And fled to heaven – set upon
A happy future there.

Fagin looked down on the boy
Without a trace of sorrow.
'Not now. Not now,' he grimly said.
'Tomorrow – yes – tomorrow.'

MR BUMBLE EARNS HIMSELF
FIVE POUNDS

Meanwhile the beadle Bumble
Had made the journey down
From his home and all the way
To sprawling London town.

He'd come on Parish business
And thought it quite a caper,
Until one day he noticed
While reading the newspaper…

A little piece that offered
Five pounds as a reward,
(A very decent sum indeed –
To some a handsome hoard)…

For information leading to
The finding of a lad.
The boy in question's name was there
Contained within the ad;

'Oliver Twist,' the beadle read,
And then there was some more.
Details of the suit of clothes
That the lost boy wore.

And right there at the very end
Was Mr Brownlow's name,
And his address – and the fine ad
Was set within a frame.

It said the money would be paid
To anyone who knew
Details of his history
And who could give a view…

About the young boy's character,
Quite anything at all.
The beadle sat up in surprise
And let the paper fall.

But then within five minutes
He set out with a will,
Striding on with purpose
To get to Pentonville.

He knocked on Mr Brownlow's door
And loudly did declaim
The purpose of his visit
And gave the young lad's name.

Mrs Bedwin let him in
And then burst into tears,
Convinced the stranger who'd arrived
Would now allay her fears.

She showed the beadle courteously
Into the parlour where
Brownlow sat with Grimwig,
Each in a comfy chair.

They had their drinks before them,
Then Mr Grimwig said,
'A parish beadle, I declare
Or I will eat my head.'

Now Brownlow spoke to Bumble,
'Pray sir, please take a seat.'
And once the usual pleasantries
Were done and quite complete…

He said, 'You are a beadle sir?'
And Bumble bowed his head.
'I'm a parochial beadle,'
Fat Bumble proudly said.

Mr Brownlow pursed his lips
And said, 'Now sir, you claim
To know about the little boy
Who goes now by the name…

'Of Oliver Twist – so pray good sir
Tell everything you know.'
The beadle folded his fat arms,
Inclined his head down low…

And he commenced his story.
He said, 'Right from his birth
He proved to be a vicious child
Of very dubious worth.

'He was a foundling sir and born
Of parents very low,
And I believe my duty
Is to let you know…

'That he's a most ungrateful child,
And quite malicious too,
And full of treachery – plain bad.
A villain through and through.

'And I must also tell you,
Though it is sad to say,
Though he was given every chance
He chose to run away.

'The boy is just a little rogue.
I'm sorry but it's true.
I hope he hasn't caused you grief
Or brought distress to you.'

Mr Brownlow sighed a sigh
As heavy we must say,
As any he had ever sighed
On any other day.

'I fear it is all true,' he said,
And took from in his coat
A spanking new and crispy
Crackling five pound note.

He handed it to Bumble
And said, 'I tell you sir
I'm very, very sorry
The boy's been proved a cur.

'For if you'd said the opposite
I would have handed you
Three times the sum I've given,
And done it gladly too.'

Bumble's face looked quite perplexed;
He scratched his balding head,
And then he huffed and puffed a bit –
And then he turned bright red.

He pocketed the fiver
But it's completely true,
If he'd known Brownlow's wish – he would
Have aired a different view.

Mr Brownlow rang his bell.
Mrs Bedwin then appeared.
He said, 'I have to sadly say
It is just as I feared.

'The boy's an arch impostor.'
'It can't be true,' she said.
'I tell you that he is,' he cried
And bowed his white haired head.

'I never will believe it sir,'
Good Mrs Bedwin cried.
'It's true,' said Mr Grimwig.
'The boy just lied and lied.'

Mrs Bedwin shouted out,
'He was a gentle child,
And very grateful too and had
A character so mild.

'I know what children are, good sir
And have for forty years.'
She spoke with resolution
Through wet and flowing tears.

'And folk who cannot claim the same
Shouldn't say a word.'
This was aimed at Grimwig who
Made out he hadn't heard.

Then Mr Brownlow yelled out loud.
'Silence,' he exclaimed.
'It's very clear the two-faced boy
Was never what he claimed.

'So do not let me hear his name.
Not today – or ever.
I rang to tell you this right now.
Do you hear me – never!'

As he spoke it was so clear
He was engulfed in gloom.
And then he said, 'I mean it too –
You may now leave the room.'

And as the dark crept on that day
I think we must concede
That in the quiet Brownlow house
There were sad hearts indeed.

OLIVER IS TAKEN TO BILL SIKES

Oliver found when he awoke
A strong new pair of shoes,
And Fagin then was standing by
To give alarming news.

'New shoes for you my dear,' he said.
'I hope they're not too tight.
And you'll be going off to stay
With Mr Sikes tonight.'

'To stay there sir?' asked Oliver.
His voice was full of fear.
Fagin said, 'Don't be afraid.
It's not for long my dear.

'We shouldn't like to give you up.
You shall come back again.'
And then he stared with such intent,
As if to make it plain…

That what he was about to say
Was of such great import,
That Oliver should listen well
To all he did exhort.

'Take heed. Take heed young Oliver,'
The withered old man said.
'Listen well to all I say
Or you may end up dead.'

He shook his hand before him
In a warning way,
And said, 'If you upset Bill Sikes
There'll be a price to pay,

'For he's a rough man through and through,
And gives no thought to blood.
When his is up – he'll easily
Bring more on like a flood.

'And so do everything he bids
And keep your thoughts locked in.'
Then Fagin's face relaxed and spread
Into a ghastly grin.

And then he softly left the room
And Oliver sank back;
He trembled there for he was sure
His future looked most black.

He fell upon his knees to pray.
His heart was filled with fear.
He felt that something awful
Was looming very near.

When he was finished he just sat
Immobile – with his head
Buried in his hands and filled
With awful, clinging dread.

Hours passed by, then Oliver
Looked up and there he saw
A silent figure standing
Over by the door.

'Who's there?' he cried in panic.
Whoever could it be?
A shaking voice then answered.
'It's me – it's only me.'

Oliver raised the candle
High into the air.
The light fell on the figure.
'Twas Nancy standing there.

'Put down the light now Oliver.'
She said, 'It hurts my eyes.'
And then she sank into a chair
With heavy, troubled sighs.

She wrung her hands and cried out loud,
'Oh God forgive me please.'
She rocked around and dropped her head
Right down between her knees.

Poor Oliver was most alarmed.
'Whatever's wrong?' he cried.
Nancy sat up, smoothed her skirt,
Looked up at him and sighed.

And then she burst out laughing.
It was a manic sound.
She beat her hands upon her legs
And stamped upon the ground.

Then suddenly she stopped and sat
With manner bleak and dire,
Silently and shivering,
Just staring at the fire.

Then finally she looked around,
Arranged her crumpled dress,
And said, to possibly allay
Young Oliver's distress…

'I don't know what gets into me.'
Her voice now sounded steady.
'It must be this damp, dirty room.
Now Nolly, are you ready?'

'Am I to go with you?' he asked.
She said, 'I've come from Bill.
And you're to come with me right now.'
Oliver stood still.

He was so frightened, terrified.
He stared down at the floor,
And then he said – recoiling,
With trembling voice, 'What for?'

'What for?' the girl then echoed.
'Oh for no harm,' she lied
And then she motioned Oliver
To step with her outside.

He said, 'I don't believe it,
Whatever you may say.'
Nancy laughed and then replied,
'Well have it your own way.

'Hush,' she said and looked around,
Then pointed to the door.
'I've tried to help you Nolly
But I can't do much more,

'For you are hedged in round and round
By misery and crime,
And if you are to get away,
Well, this is not the time.

'I've saved you once from injury,
And will, I'm sure, again.
If someone else had fetched you
They would have caused you pain,

'For they are rough – their anger
Is very quick to riot,
But I have promised them you'll be
A good boy and come quiet.

'And if you don't I promise you,'
She spoke with gasping breath.
'You'll do great harm unto yourself
And maybe cause my death.

'See here! I've borne all this for you.
Bill's violent when he chooses.'
She pointed to her arms and neck
And showed him ugly bruises.

'Remember these,' she cried, distressed,
'Remember what you saw.
I can't do much to help you now.
Don't make me suffer more…

'For they don't mean to do you harm.
For now just let it be.
So hush – for every word from you
Just means a blow for me.

'Now Oliver – give me your hand.'
She then blew out the light
And led him down the creaking stairs
And out into the night.

A carriage waited there outside.
Nancy whispered, 'Hush.'
They boarded, then the driver's whip
Lashed out – and in a rush…

They set off down the darkened street
And at enormous speed,
And as they went, with curtains closed
Nancy told him 'Heed!'

She carried on remorselessly.
And yes, she even swore,
And poured out all the warnings
She'd given him before.

Finally Bill Sikes's house
Came bleakly into sight.
The one that Fagin visited
On the previous night.

For one brief moment Oliver
Looked along the street
To see if there was anyone
That he could thus entreat…

To save him from these awful folk,
But there was no-one near,
And still the girl's beseeching voice
Was sounding in his ear…

Reminding him what would occur
If he just ran away,
For it could mean a beating or
Bring on her final day.

And so he stayed just where he was.
He didn't have the heart
To try to run away – escape,
Abandon her – depart.

Nancy led him to the door.
Oliver went as bid.
And then he heard Bill Sikes yell out,
'So 'ave yer got the kid?'

'Yes here he is,' said Nancy.
'He came just like a lamb.'
'I'm pleased to 'ear it,' Sikes replied.
'I'm glad of that I am.

'For if it had been otherwise,
'Twould have bin bad for 'im.'
Then he addressed scared Oliver
With face all set and grim.

'It's time we 'ad a little talk.
It's best we get it done.'
And saying this he pointed to
An evil looking gun.

'Now do yer know wot this is then?'
Oliver said, 'Yes.'
He stood quite rigid – inwardly
He shook in great distress.

Sikes began to load the gun.
When this was done he said,
'Stand up close' and then he pressed
The gun to the boy's head.

'Now if you speak a word at all
Once we are out about,
Or even worse if you begin
To make a fuss or shout…

'Well know this gun is loaded.'
And then foul Bill Sikes cursed,
And said, 'If you've a mind for that,
Well say your last prayer first.'

He turned away and Oliver
As best as he was able
Composed himself – and Nancy there
Quickly laid the table.

They had a meagre supper
And Sikes downed lots of gin,
The way he drank did not improve
The mood that he was in.

Then Sikes sent Oliver to bed –
They had an early start.
Oliver lay there wide awake
With very heavy heart.

And Nancy sat there staring
Into the withering fire,
For she'd been tasked with waking them
And so did not retire.

Oliver thought that she might take
The opportunity
To whisper some advice to him,
But she sat wearily…

Just brooding there before the fire.
Sat in a crumpled heap,
And as for Oliver, well he
Soon fell fast asleep.

When he awoke it was still dark
And heavy, driving rain
Was pouring down outside and beat
Against the window pane.

'Now then,' growled Sikes, 'It's half past five.'
In an impatient state.
'Look sharp and get some breakfast
For we are running late.'

While Oliver ate his scanty meal,
Nancy, looking grim,
Just stared into the fire absorbed
And hardly looked at him.

Then Sikes gave Oliver a cape.
A rough and dirty one.
And then he drew his own cape back
And showed the boy his gun.

A farewell then to Nancy
And Sikes was out the door.
Oliver, as he followed
Looked at the girl once more.

He hoped their eyes would meet but she
With vacant, sombre stare
Sat in her place before the fire,
Just rocking in her chair.

THE EXPEDITION

It was a cheerless morning
When they got to the street,
With stormy clouds, so menacing,
And blowing, driving sleet.

Puddles lay upon the ground
And in the early light
It was apparent, lots of rain
Had fallen in the night.

Sikes made his way through Shoreditch
And on through Sun Street too;
Down Crown Street and 'cross Finsbury Square,
Then Smithfield came in view.

It was a market morning,
The ground was just aflood
With reeking filth and mire and all
And ankle-deep in mud.

And thick steam rose perpetually
From cattle packed in there,
And sheep were penned in too and folk
Were shoving everywhere.

Countrymen and butchers,
Drovers, hawkers too.
Thieves, vagabonds and idlers –
Just one great, heaving stew.

Sikes dragged young Oliver along
Through all this muddled mess.
The boy just followed on – borne down
With anguish and distress.

Occasionally Sikes nodded
To someone that he knew,
Then hurried on through Hosier Lane
Till Holborn came in view.

'Now, young 'un,' Sikes said angrily,
'Don't lag behind already.'
Poor Oliver was feeling tired.
His legs felt quite unsteady.

But Sikes just yanked him on and so
He kept up best he could.
They passed on through to Mayfair –
A classy neighbourhood.

Past Hyde Park Corner – on they went,
To Kensington, and there
They saw a man upon a cart
Pulled by a frisky mare.

And written on the cart they saw,
'Hounslow' – so Bill Sikes said,
'Can we 'ave a lift then mate?'
The man inclined his head.

'Jump up,' he then replied and so
In one beat of a heart
Sikes and tired, young Oliver
Jumped up onto the cart.

They travelled on and journeyed through
Hammersmith – Chiswick too,
And everywhere they went it seemed
Was somewhere that Sikes knew.

Across Kew Bridge to Brentford,
Till finally they came
Upon a run-down public house
Called by the common name…

Of 'The Coach and Horses':
They bid the man goodbye;
Oliver could only raise
A heavy, awkward sigh.

'He's sulky,' Bill Sikes then explained
With manner mean and grim.
'He's just a spoilt and sulky dog.
Don't give no mind to 'im.'

'Not I,' the man replied and smiled.
'For it's a lovely day.'
And then he cracked his whip and drove
Quite happily away.

Then on they walked through Twickenham.
To Hampton by the river.
Occasionally Sikes touched his gun
Which caused a frightened shiver…

To deeply surge through Oliver –
It gave him such a scare.
Sikes did it just to let him know
The gun was still right there.

Finally they reached a pub –
A scruffy run-down hole.
It seemed this nondescript old place
Had been Bill Sikes's goal.

They had some meat for dinner,
Then Oliver fell asleep.
He was so tired he just collapsed
Into a tangled heap.

When he awoke he heard Bill Sikes
Deep in a conversation.
Oliver listened wearily
But with rapt concentration.

'So you're bound for Lower Halliford?'
Bill Sikes was now saying.
Oliver heard it clearly from
The spot where he was laying.

'Yes I am,' the man replied
A little worse for wear,
For he'd been drinking heavily
And had a bloodshot stare.

'Now you could give my boy an' me
A lift in your nice cart.'
Sikes pushed some ale towards the man
Who sat up with a start.

'You goin' then to Halliford?'
The man asked as he drank.
'Twas obvious he'd had a few
Because his breathing stank.

'We're heading on to Shepperton,'
Sikes said – his voice was low.
'Well I'm yer man,' the drunk replied
'As far as I do go.'

And then he asked how much he owed
To a buxom maid.
She replied, 'It's settled for
This 'ere man has paid.'

'I say,' he said with gravity.
'Why that will never do.'
'Why not?' said Sikes, 'wot's wrong if I
Stand you a pint or two…

'For you are giving us a lift.'
The drunk let out a bellow,
And then declared, 'You surely are
A first-class, top-notch fellow.'

And so they went outside and then
Made ready to depart.
They climbed onto the drunken man's
Decrepit wooden cart.

And off they drove in silence.
The driver, full of drink –
Didn't talk – he reeked of booze.
He gave off quite a stink.

And Sikes was in no mood to talk,
And Oliver – down at heart,
Just huddled in a corner of
The slowly moving cart.

The night was dark and freezing cold.
A wind blew sharp and keen.
And branches of gaunt trees were cowed
To mould a sombre scene.

So all was desolation –
The driver on his perch
With Sikes beside him, in a mood
As they passed Sunbury church.

Two or three miles further on
The horses rhythmic clop
Came to an end and now the cart
Came slowly to a stop.

Oliver and Sikes jumped down.
They said a quick goodbye,
And then they walked into the night
Beneath a morbid sky.

Finally they reached a bridge
And turned down by a bank,
And Oliver's fast beating heart
Now fearfully just sank.

Sick with fear and trembling.
His mind confused and fraught.
'He's brought me to this lonely place
To murder me,' he thought.

He was about to try his best
To ward off Sikes's knife.
One last attempt to struggle for
His young, neglected life…

When there before him he espied
Standing all alone,
A ruinous, decaying house.
A dark mass on its own.

It looked quite uninhabited
As Sikes approached the door.
He raised the latch and quietly
To himself, he swore.

The door yielded then before him.
He pushed it open wide,
And pulling Oliver behind
Bill Sikes then stepped inside.

THE BURGLARY

'Hallo there,' a voice called out.
Sikes's face grew tight.
'Don't make a row for heavens sake.
And Toby show a light.'

'It's my old pal,' the voice replied.
It came from in the rear.
'It's Bill Sikes in the passageway.
Barney – do you hear?

'Wake up you dog and bring him in
Or I'll wake you all right.'
Barney roused himself and then
Stumbled with a light.

He greeted Sikes with cheerfulness.
'Come in. Come in, now sir.'
He said this very pleasantly
As if he would infer…

That he was pleased to see them,
As was indeed the case,
For he'd been wondering for a while
If Bill would show his face.

Sikes pushed scared Oliver along
Through the dismal gloom,
And then they entered cautiously
A low and darkened room.

A smoky fire was burning.
The room was pretty bare.
Just scruffy , broken furniture –
And sitting in a chair…

A man lounged puffing on a pipe,
Smoke swirling round his head.
He turned, upon them entering,
'Well Bill, my boy,' he said.

'I'd almost given up on you.'
And then he gave a cry,
And said, 'Well Bill, just who is this?'
Sikes said – and with a sigh…

'Just a boy. Yeah, just a boy.
He's one of Fagin's crew.'
Toby Crackit – for 'twas his name,
Replied, 'Well, he should do.'

And then he looked at Oliver,
His face all taut and grim.
'Just see his pretty mug,' he said.
''Twill make a mint for him.

'When he picks old lady's pockets
'Twill seem beyond belief
That someone with a face like that
Could ever be a thief.'

Bill Sikes then sat himself right down
To rest his aching feet.
He said, 'While we are waiting
I'd like something to eat.'

And then he gave fraught Oliver
Another massive fright.
He said, 'Sit down and rest yerself
For later on tonight…

'We're goin' out again – although
We won't be goin' far.'
Oliver looked at Sikes askance –
He felt way under par.

His head was aching terribly.
His thoughts a jumbled maze.
He dropped his head into his hands
Just in a muddled daze.

Then Toby Crackit drank a toast
And slapped Bill on the back.
He laughed out loud and then exclaimed,
'Success to this fine crack.'

He downed his glass in one and Sikes
Did the very same.
It seemed they were amused as if
The whole thing were a game.

Then Toby filled another glass
And cried out once again,
'It's down with innocence I say –
So give the boy a drain.'

He gave a glass to Oliver.
He said, 'Now drink yer fill,
For I know what is good fer you.
Tell him to drink it Bill.'

'He'd better drink it,' Sikes exclaimed.
'Oh he's a perverse one.'
And as he spoke he clapped his hand
On where he kept his gun.

Oliver was frightened now.
He drank the contents down.
Then in an instant his small face
Took on a ghastly frown.

And then he started coughing
In such a violent way
That he was overcome with fear,
Concern and deep dismay.

But Toby Crackit, Barney too,
Those two unruly tykes,
Just laughed out loud – a smile too crossed
The face of mean Bill Sikes.

Then after they had eaten
They settled down to nap.
Oliver slept upon a stool,
His hands laid in his lap.

The motley crew all fell asleep
And slept for quite a while,
Till Toby jumping up declared
In his remorseless style…

'It's half past one. It's time to go.'
They swiftly all awoke
And drew their greatcoats on – they looked
Like menacing, rough folk.

Which was exactly what they were
For Toby now drew out
Some pistols from the cupboard then,
Spoke with a cocky shout;

'These are the persuaders.'
Which made the others laugh.
Bill Sikes then said, 'They'll do the job.
I'm telling you – not 'arf.'

'Have we got everything we need?'
Asked Toby – that cut-throat –
And as he spoke he stashed away
A crowbar in his coat.

'Now then,' said Sikes, 'Let's be away.
Oliver – take my 'and.'
And then the robbers stepped outside –
A small but ruthless band.

Barney stayed behind and so
Once they had left the house,
He curled up as before and slept
As quiet as a mouse.

And as for little Oliver,
Well he was dragged along
By the two fearsome villains who
Were powerful and strong.

The fog was heavier than before –
Though damp, no rain fell down,
And as they walked on briskly
They soon reached Chertsey town.

'We'll go right through the 'eart of it,'
Said Sikes with little fuss.
'There'll be no-one around at all
To spot or trouble us.

'This town does not require to be
Avoided – even skirted,
Because at this late time of night
The whole place is deserted.'

How right he was, for nobody
Was anywhere about.
Just an occasional dog barked and
A bedroom light shone out.

They cleared the town just as they heard
The church clock strike out two.
They walked on quickly then until
A wall came into view.

It was constructed round a house.
A solid home of brick.
And Toby climbed right up the wall
In just the merest tick.

'The boy can come up next,' he hissed.
'Hoist him and I'll catch hold.'
And in a tick Bill Sikes had done
Just what he had been told.

In seconds, nothing more for sure,
Bill Sikes with strength and stealth
Pushed Oliver across the wall
And then scaled it himself.

They dropped down on the other side
And Oliver now saw,
With absolute, clear certainty
They planned to break the law.

For robbery and housebreaking,
Or maybe murder too,
Seemed to be the actions that
The rough pair planned to do.

He clasped his hands in horror
And sighed such awful sighs,
And cold sweat ran upon his face,
A mist came to his eyes.

His legs sank then beneath him,
He fell onto his knees.
His poor, scared mind was crying out
With silent, grieving pleas.

Bill Sikes was not the kind of man
To let such action pass.
He said, 'Get up or else I'll strew
Yer brains across the grass.'

'For heavens sake just let me go,'
Came Oliver's wild cry.
'Just let me run away and go
Into a field and die.

'I'll never come near London town.'
And then a fraught appeal.
'Oh pray have mercy on me sir.
And please don't make me steal.'

Sikes swore a dreadful oath and then
He cocked his evil gun,
But Toby struck the gun and said
He wouldn't see it done.

'Hush,' he cried. 'That's not the way.
I'll see to it instead.
Not like that – but with a crack
Across the wretch's head.

'It's just as certain but genteel,
But I now think we'll find
The kid has come around and now
Has changed his awkward mind.'

Sikes cursed old Fagin there and then
For choosing from his boys,
This surly rogue who moaned and groaned
And made a deal of noise.

Then Toby said, 'The crowbar Bill –
It's there with all our gear.
'Twill force this shutter open wide,
So bring it over here.'

He spoke about a window as
He shiftily turned round –
Located at the house's rear,
Just five feet from the ground.

It was quite undefended.
It seemed the owners thought
That an attempt to penetrate
Would surely come to naught.

But this was really not the case
And surely most unwise,
For there was room for somebody
Of Oliver's small size.

In moments Sikes had loosened
The shutter – it now stood
Open wide and Sikes declared
From 'neath his darkened hood…

'Now listen, yer young, worthless limb,
I'm putting you through there.
So take this light and move yerself,
And mind yer take good care.

'Go along the little hall
And don't make any din.
And then undo the outside door
So you can let us in.'

And Toby said, 'You'll find a bolt
At the top somewhere.
You'll never reach it on your own
So stand upon a chair.'

Then Bill Sikes lowered Oliver
With care, into the house.
Then said, 'Now take the lantern,
Be quiet as a mouse.'

He pointed to the outside door
With his black, nasty gun,
And said, 'I'll shoot yer good an' dead
If yer try to run.

'Yer dead in just a minute
If yer try to shirk.
A soon as I let go of you,
Then go and do yer work.'

'What's that?' then Toby whispered.
They listened very hard,
But not a sound was heard within
The house or in the yard.

'Right do it now,' Bill Sikes declared.
He let the scared boy go.
But Oliver had decided
To let the inmates know.

For he was firmly now resolved
He wouldn't sneak or creep,
But he would dart right up the stairs
And rouse them from their sleep.

As Oliver began to walk
He heard Bill Sikes breathe out,
'Get back over 'ere, yer cur.'
With angry, muffled shout.

Poor Oliver was really scared
Hearing this fierce cry.
He didn't know what he should do.
Advance, stay still or fly.

He dropped the lantern on the floor.
A light appeared and then
He saw a vision up above –
Two frightened, half-dressed men.

And then there was a blinding flash.
Some smoke – a noisy crack.
And then his world went hazy
And then he staggered back.

He'd been hit by a bullet,
And as his poor arm bled,
'Twas lucky he was still alive
Not on the floor, stone dead.

He stood beneath the window,
Shocked and in distress,
He saw that things had turned into
A really awful mess.

Sikes's face had disappeared
But now appeared once more.
He fired his pistol at the men,
And angrily he swore.

He leant then through the window,
Now of just one mind
To get a hold of Oliver,
So grabbed him from behind.

He yanked him by the collar,
And pulled him off the ground,
Then through the window – then he yelled.
A loud and piercing sound.

'They've hit him. Quick. Damnation.
My how the boy does bleed.'
Poor Oliver was out of it
And gave the words scant heed.

He heard the ringing of a bell.
The shouting of scared men.
The noise of fire-arms going off –
And the sensation then…

Of being carried 'cross the ground
And at a rapid pace.
And then a deathly feeling
Passed slowly o'er his face.

And coldness crept across his heart
And gripped it like a claw.
And then he slipped into a trance
And saw and heard no more.

OLIVER'S CONTINUING ADVENTURES

'Wolves tear yer throats,' cried Sikes out loud,
As he, with fear, looked back.
He peered to see, but all behind
Was misty – inky black.

He laid the bleeding Oliver
Across his bended knee,
And looked with concentration
To see what he could see.

He could discern but little
As he crouched staring there,
Then the shouting out of men
Vibrated through the air.

And barking out of nearby dogs
Roused by the great alarm
Seemed to confirm that if they could,
They'd cause a deal of harm.

'Stop, yer lily livered hound,'
Sikes shouted out with rage.
Toby Crackit ceased to run
Then did his best to gauge…

Was he in range of pistol shot?
He looked and thought, 'I am.'
And he could see that Bill's black mood
Was not an idle sham.

Oh no – for he was in a rage.
It surely was no ploy.
Sikes roared again, 'You – come back 'ere
And help me with the boy.'

Reluctantly scared Toby then
Made something of a show,
In going back despite the fact
He didn't want to know.

Sikes cried out, 'Come back, yer tyke.
Don't play the booby there.'
But then the sound of voices
Came crackling 'cross the air.

'It's all up Bill,' cried Toby then.
'It's time we ran and hid.
Show 'em your heels and quickly –
And drop the useless kid.'

And then he turned and ran away
At an enormous speed.
And now Sikes too began to think
And also then took heed.

For now he saw his mate was right.
It was no time to stay.
He saw that he would soon be caught
Unless he ran away.

He threw the bleeding Oliver
Onto the muddy ground,
Then ran towards a leafy hedge
And cleared it with a bound.

And though the men were running hard
And swiftly coming on,
Bill Sikes had disappeared from sight.
He'd well and truly gone.

And so those evil robbers,
The dregs of all mankind,
Got away but coldly left
Poor Oliver behind.

And those who'd chased them now gave up
And slowly headed back.
The robbers had quite disappeared
Into the night's deep black.

The dreadful night wore slowly on
And with approaching day,
The air grew colder – damper too –
And there the poor boy lay.

The mist rolled on across the ground,
Just like a cloud of smoke.
It settled on the freezing earth
Like a translucent cloak.

The grass was soaking wet and cold.
And on the small pathway
All was damp and reeking mire –
And there the poor boy lay.

He lay where Sikes had left him,
Right on the very spot.
Abandoned by the evil thief –
Thrown on the ground to rot.

He lay there quite insensible
With ashen, lifeless face.
As he became much weaker still
The dawn grew on apace.

But rather than the birth of day,
'Twas more the death of night
That faintly glimmered in the sky
To bring the morning light.

Gentle rays traversed the sky;
The coming of the day,
Which brought a glow to everything
In its uplifting way.

Objects that looked terrible
In the dead of night
Now gradually resolved into
Things that looked all right.

The rain came down and fell upon
The leafless bushes there.
It pattered down and noisily,
And echoed through the air.

It beat upon still Oliver
In a remorseless way
As he lay there unconscious
Upon a bed of clay.

But then a cry came from him,
And then a mournful croak,
And uttering it, the wretched boy
Quite suddenly awoke.

His injured arm was tied in rag
And covered all in mud.
It hung down at his side and was
Covered too – in blood.

He was so weak, he found it hard
To raise himself at all.
He lay there looking frail and ill
And very, very small.

But finally he managed,
By leaning on one hand,
To sit upright and then he tried
To raise himself and stand.

He trembled with exhaustion
And made a crying sound,
Then shuddering from head to toe
He fell back to the ground.

He lay there on the sodden earth –
Let out a woeful sigh,
But then he thought, 'If I stay here,
I'll very likely die.'

And so he staggered to his feet
And stumbled to and fro.
Just like a drunken, sodden man
He knew not where to go.

But still he tottered onwards –
He did his very best.
His head was drooping languidly
Upon his heaving chest.

He stumbled on as if borne down
By a tremendous load;
Across a field and down a lane
Until he reached a road.

And there he saw not far away
Through a line of beech,
A house that he now hoped and prayed
He just, perhaps, could reach.

And surely if they saw his face,
Pale, forlorn and ashen,
They just might be encouraged to
Show him some compassion.

And if they failed him – 'Well,' he thought,
With a heavy sigh.
'At least I'll be near human folk
When it comes time to die.'

And so he summoned all his strength
For this one final trial.
The house was surely not too far.
No more than half a mile.

But then as he approached it,
He heaved a wretched sob,
For the house turned out to be
The one they'd tried to rob.

It was without a trace of doubt
The house he'd seen last night,
And though his arm was agony,
His mind turned now to flight.

But flight to where? Where could he go?
His thoughts were so forlorn.
He pushed the garden gate and then
Staggered 'cross the lawn.

He climbed the steps and faintly knocked
Upon the large front door,
And then collapsed in front of it –
Exhausted to his core.

~ ~ ~

Now in the house, at this time –
Putting the world to right –
Were those who'd chased the robbers
Upon the previous night.

They were a servant, Mr Giles;
Another known as Brittles;
A tinker who'd been passing through,
Had joined them at their vittles.

Despite the fact they'd given chase
Till they were out of breath,
It didn't change the fact at all
That they'd been scared to death.

But now proud Mr Giles sat there –
Legs outstretched by the fire,
And though but just a servant
You'd think he was a squire.

He spoke about the robbery
To the housemaid and the cook,
And how he'd tried his level best
To bring the thieves to book.

And just how brave young Brittles was,
And how they could be dead.
'I should have died had it been me,'
The frightened housemaid said.

'Well, you're a woman,' Brittles smiled.
'This is beyond your ken.'
'Aye, that is right,' said Mr Giles.
'This was a job for men.

'For ladies aren't expected
To be as brave as us.
Oh no – the little ladies
Are wont to make a fuss;

'But we knew there was work to do,
So would we back away?
Cower in a corner and
Drop on our knees and pray.

'No, off we went to apprehend
Those robbers in the night.'
But Mr Giles then started,
And anxiously, with fright.

Oh yes, he stopped his swaggering
And acting like a bore,
For everyone had heard it too –
A faint knock on the door.

'It was a knock,' said Mr Giles,
Pretending to be calm.
He acted with serenity
To cover his alarm.

'Someone – open up the door.'
Nobody moved an inch.
And then the knock was heard again
And caused them all to flinch.

'The door must now be answered.'
Scared Giles spoke out again,
But judging by the frightened looks
His words were said in vain.

He looked at Brittles pleadingly
But Brittles shied away.
The tinker too was quite intent
That he would sit and stay.

And then the timid Mr Giles
Said, 'Tell you what we'll do,
We'll all go there together.
Yes me – and you and you.'

He pointed at the tinker
And Brittles – and he swore
That surely they'd be brave enough
To open up the door.

And so with this persuasion
They stepped into the hall,
Each filled with trepidation
At what might now befall.

They held each other firmly,
And now no sound was heard,
Then Mr Giles composed himself
And then he gave the word.

'Right – open up the door,' he said.
He squeezed poor Brittles wrist.
They pulled the door ajar to see –
Poor little Oliver Twist.

He lay there quite exhausted,
With just no strength to rise,
And all that he could manage was
To raise his heavy eyes.

'A boy,' cried Mr Giles out loud.
'Why Brittles look down here.
Well indeed, I never did.
Well this is really queer.'

Brittles looked at Oliver
And then he loudly swore,
For recognition dawned on him
From the night before.

When Mr Giles saw Oliver
He grabbed a hold of him.
Thankfully he didn't seize
His blood soaked, injured limb.

'Here he is,' he bawled out loud
Right in the poor boy's face.
'Here's one of them there thieves, dear ma'am'
He yelled up the staircase.

A youthful lady had appeared.
'Hush.' – Her plea was curt.
'You'll frighten my poor aunt again –
Now tell me, is he hurt?'

'He's wounded desperately, sweet ma'am,'
Said Giles complacently.
'Well, wait a moment,' came reply.
'Just hang on there for me.

'For I must speak with my dear aunt.'
And then she tripped away.
And when she came back she announced
That the boy could stay.

'Take him carefully up to bed.
And then good Giles take heed.
Fetch the doctor and the police.
And do it with all speed.'

'But won't you take a look first miss,'
Said Mr Giles with pride.
It overcame him totally –
He didn't try to hide…

Just how pleased he was to catch
A thief from out of town.
He felt puffed up as if he'd brought
A rare and fine bird down.

'Not for the world,' replied the girl.
'It makes my poor heart break.
Oh treat him kindly Mr Giles,
If only for my sake.'

The servant gazed up at the lass.
His thoughts were all awhirl.
His glance as fond as if she'd been
His very own sweet girl.

Then bending over Oliver,
Free of his former cares,
He carried the poor, suffering boy,
With gentleness, upstairs.

OLIVER'S NEW ACQUAINTANCES

In a handsome room that was
Old fashioned in its way,
Sat two fine ladies breakfasting
Upon the following day;

And Mr Giles was there as well
Dressed in a suit of black –
In attendance while they ate
Their tasty morning snack.

He stood there motionless between
The sideboard and the table,
Intent to show the ladies there
That only he was able…

To be attentive to their needs –
He stood there tall, erect;
And as he did his sense of worth
Seemed thus to go unchecked.

His head thrown back, inclined a tad,
His left leg just advanced,
His right hand in his waistcoat and
His being thus enhanced…

By such an air of self regard,
His manner seemed to say
He thought he was of great import
In every single way.

One dear lady was quite old –
And this was plain to see.
As she sat in an upright chair –
Not more upright than she!

She sat in stately manner,
Her still sharp eyes upon
The younger lady seated there,
Whose bright eyes also shone.

A lovely girl just in the bloom
Of springtime womanhood,
Her every look and movement told
That she was sweet and good.

She was no more than seventeen
And in her deep blue eyes
There beamed a rare intelligence
That bordered on the wise.

The thousand lights that played upon
Her happy, lovely face
Left no room for shadows there –
No, not the slightest trace.

Then the elder lady smiled.
She said, 'So tell me please,
How long since Brittles went to fetch
The doctor from his ease?'

Mr Giles looked at his watch.
'An hour, maybe more.'
But as he spoke a gentleman
Came flying through the door.

Somehow he'd got into the house –
Not bothering to ring.
He cried, 'I've never, ever heard
Of such an awful thing…

'Mrs Maylie, bless my soul,
And in the dead of night.'
He shook both ladies by the hand.
'You should be dead from fright.

'You should have called for me, my dear,
And all so unexpected.
What an awful, dreadful thing
To which you've been subjected.

'And in the silence of the night.
I don't know what to say.'
And so the doctor carried on
In his eccentric way.

The thing that seemed to tax him most
Was that the robbery
Was unexpected and at night –
How did he think 'twould be?

Did he think that the gentlemen –
In their housebreaking way –
Would transact such business calls
At noon – in light of day?

Or maybe send out prior word
By the Twopenny post,
To give fair notice of their call
To their reluctant host.

'And you Miss Rose, my dear, sweet girl.
Are you all right?' he cried.
'I'm fine, I'm fine,' she whispered,
And then she sadly sighed.

'But there's a poor dear creature
In our spare room upstairs
Who isn't well and is brought down
With injuries and cares.'

'Ah to be sure,' the doctor mouthed,
Then said, 'I understand
The injuries the boy sustained
Came from good Giles's hand.'

Mr Giles, he cleared his throat
And blushed the brightest red,
And shuffled rather awkwardly
And proudly he then said,

'Yes I have had that honour sir.'
The doctor sighed, 'Well now.
Honour eh? Well I don't know.'
But to avoid a row…

He said 'Where is this robber then?
Giles – please show the way.'
And Mr Giles did as he asked.
He had no more to say.

The doctor said, 'I will stop by
Mrs Maylie dear,
On my way back down again,
And Rose, please have no fear,

'And well my very goodness me.'
He spoke with puzzled grin.
'That little window over there.
Is that how he got in?'

And so he followed Giles upstairs
Just talking all the time,
But in a pleasant, homely way
That's surely not a crime.

Now Dr Losberne was his name
And he was fat and round.
In every action that he took
Great kindness did abound.

And though it could be true to say
Upon initial meeting
That Losberne had grown fat and wide
From massive over-eating,

This really wouldn't have been true
But just an unkind rumour,
For he'd grown large and mostly from
His kind and hearty humour.

Oh yes, his only problem was
A habit of just giving.
He really didn't overeat
Or have too much good living.

The doctor stayed with Oliver
For really quite a while
But finally he reappeared
And said with measured guile,

'This is quite extraordinary.'
Then Mrs Maylie said,
'He's not in danger is he?
Or worse than that, not dead.'

The doctor reassured her
Which came as a relief,
And then he said, 'Now tell me ma'am
Have you observed this thief?'

'No,' replied the lady.
'I have not seen the lad,
But think I must assume the fact
That he is very bad.'

'Well you must come and see him,'
The doctor then replied.
'Well if you think we really should,'
The sweet old lady sighed.

And so they climbed the wooden stairs –
Up to the bedroom door.
Good Dr Losberne raised his hand
And then he spoke once more.

He spoke in muffled whisper,
'Let's see now what you think.'
And then he opened up the door
By just a little chink.

He checked to see that all was calm
Then motioned them inside;
Advancing then towards the bed
He threw its curtains wide.

Upon it lay no ruffian
All evil, black and base.
Instead they saw a battered child,
So innocent of face.

He lay worn with exhaustion.
His wounded arm bound well.
He was asleep – was comfortable
As far as one could tell.

Young Rose then glided softly past
And sat beside the bed.
She gently gathered his long hair
And smoothed it o'er his head.

And as she did great teardrops fell.
She couldn't help but weep.
And then they saw the wretched boy
Smile softly in his sleep.

It was as though these gentle marks
Of pity and compassion
Had wakened dreams of love and care
Upon that face so ashen.

And maybe now he dreamt such dreams
As he had never known,
Of gentle music, or at large
In woodland, on his own.

Of rippling water flowing by
In a silent place.
Whatever thoughts went through his mind
Brought peace to his young face.

Mrs Maylie then exclaimed,
'Whatever can this mean?
This child can't be a robber.
I'd vow his hands are clean.'

The doctor sighed and said that vice
Took up its base abode,
In many temples on its way
Along its evil road.

'But surely you cannot believe,'
Cried Rose with flashing eyes,
'This boy has lived with robbers – no!
I can't believe such lies.'

Dr Losberne winced and said,
'We'll listen to his tale
And then decide if he deserves
To end up in a jail.'

The ladies now returned downstairs
But Dr Losberne stayed.
His doctor's caring feelings now
Were steadfastly displayed;

And so he waited patiently
For Oliver to awake,
He didn't have a clue how long
His vigil there would take.

'Twas not until the shadows
Of evening filled the house
That Dr Losberne crept downstairs
As quiet as a mouse.

He told the ladies sitting there,
'The boy is very ill,
But troubled with anxiety.
His mind will not be still.

'He wishes to disclose some things,
So ladies, come along,
For we must listen to his words,
But heed, he's still not strong.'

They went to sit with Oliver.
He told them of his past.
It took a while but finally
He lay back tired at last.

They heard about his suffering,
The catalogue of woe.
Of every awful happening.
Of each ensuing blow.

How evil men had brought him down.
How he'd been badly used.
How he'd been beaten, led astray
And generally abused.

They heard about the cruelty
And misery and all.
You wouldn't think in one short life
Such evil could befall.

When Oliver was finished
Kind hands smoothed down his bed.
His story told, he lay quite still
And rested his young head.

He fell asleep and happy dreams
Across his mind then crept,
And loveliness and virtue watched
Upon him as he slept.

On Oliver's arrival
The police had been alerted;
But now the efforts of his friends
Had quickly been concerted…

To convince the officers
That he was not a crook;
There was no cause at all to bring
The little lad to book.

So Dr Losberne used his guile
And all his wily skill
To convince the police the boy
Was innocent and ill.

And so the police became assured
That all that had occurred
Had not involved young Oliver.
They took the doctor's word.

So Oliver was left in peace
With his good-hearted friends,
Surrounded by the blessings that
A kindly heaven sends.

OLIVER RECEIVES A DISAPPOINTMENT

Oliver really wasn't well
For in addition to
His painful, damaged, broken limb,
All bloodied, bruised and blue,

He suffered from a fever
That had now taken hold,
Caused by the dire reaction of
Exposure to the cold.

But slowly he grew better
And he regained his strength;
He was so keen to help them out,
Would go to any length…

To pay them for their kindness –
He said his only goal
Was to serve them faithfully
With all his heart and soul.

Rose sighed and said, 'Well bless you dear
There's time enough for that.'
And as she spoke she leant across
And gave his head a pat.

Said Oliver, 'I feel so sad
And so ungrateful too
To Mr Brownlow and his nurse,
Oh goodness, yes I do.

'For they were very kind to me.
They opened up their door.
But if they knew I'm happy now
They would be pleased for sure.'

Mrs Maylie then spoke out,
'I know they would,' she said.
'And Dr Losberne promised me
That once you're out of bed…

'He'll take you off to visit them.'
'Oh will he?' cried the boy.
'For when I see them, I will be
Just overwhelmed with joy.'

And so it was it came to pass
One morning not long after,
That Dr Losberne was the cause
Of happy, joyful laughter.

For he announced to Oliver
A carriage was outside,
And he proposed that both of them
Should take a little ride,

And go in search of Brownlow,
And call on him that day.
Oliver was overjoyed,
And knew not what to say.

So off they went and shortly
They crossed o'er Chertsey bridge,
Then as the carriage trundled down
From off the bridge's ridge,

Young Oliver turned very pale.
'That house,' he cried with fear.
'The robber took me to that house.'
He shook as they drew near.

'The devil is it,' Losberne cried.
'Coachman – let me out.'
He tumbled from the coach with speed
And with a raucous shout.

He battered on the house's door.
A scruffy man appeared.
'What's the matter?' he exclaimed.
He didn't look afeared.

'Matter,' cried the doctor then.
My word how he did holler.
'Robbery's the matter here.'
He grabbed the shocked man's collar.

'There'll be a murder too, d'ya hear,
If you don't get off me,'
The rough man remonstrated
Struggling to get free.

'Where's that confounded fellow?
Where's Sikes? Is he in there?'
The startled man fought angrily
And gave an evil stare.

He managed then to free himself
By one almighty twist,
And then with eyes a-blazing
He swore and shook his fist.

'What do you mean by all of this?
And in the light of day.
Entering my house and in
This rough and violent way.

'So do you mean to murder me?
Or rob me of my cash?
A waste of time, I only have
A paltry little stash.'

Dr Losberne checked the rooms
But not a soul was there.
He found nobody hiding in
This so-called robber's lair.

The doctor felt embarrassed.
He thought, 'For goodness sake,
The boy has clearly got it wrong
And made a great mistake.'

He said, 'Here, have some money.'
And threw it at the man,
Then strode back to the carriage;
In fact he almost ran.

The rough man followed him with speed –
He cursed him all the time,
Denying then with every step
Involvement in a crime.

But when he reached the carriage door
He took a glance inside
And there he saw young Oliver
All frightened and wide-eyed.

He gave the boy a horrid look,
So fierce and sharp and grim
That Oliver remembered it –
For months it haunted him.

They drove away and left the man
Whose feelings were on fire.
Angry, flashing evil looks –
Self-righteous, full of ire.

The doctor now spoke to himself.
'Oh what an ass I am.
I could have got myself into
A most horrendous jam.

'For even if that house had been
The right one after all,
There is no telling just what might
Have come then to befall.

'What could I do all on my own?
I'm not a man to fight.
I could have had an awful time
And 'twould have served me right.

'I act on impulse Oliver.
It really doesn't do.
Don't do it lad – on no account,
That's my advice to you.'

Of course the worthy doctor
Had always through his life,
Acted on an impulse though
It often caused him strife.

And though he acted in this way
Upon each passing whim,
He still retained esteem, respect,
From all those close to him.

Now on they travelled in the coach –
Oliver knew the way,
And soon they reached the very street
He'd left that wretched day.

He pointed then unto a house.
'That's Mr Brownlow's there.'
The carriage stopped – they clambered down
And both began to stare.

For in the window was a sign
Which caused them both to fret,
For bold as brass the sign declared
The house was now 'To Let.'

'We'll knock there at the neighbour's house.'
The doctor spoke with force.
'For they will know his whereabouts.
They'll have been told of course.'

A servant in the next door house
Soon told them of the score.
Mr Brownlow had gone off
A month or so before.

He'd left for the West Indies.
He'd gone there with a friend.
His housekeeper had gone as well,
All three intent to spend…

A long, relaxing time abroad –
Oh dear this was a blow.
When in the world they would come back?
There was no way to know.

And so they headed homewards.
The sadness Oliver felt
Was overpowering, cruel and deep –
He felt that he'd been dealt…

Another awful, bitter blow,
For he'd spent days and nights,
Reflecting on the special joy
And all the great delights…

Of seeing them and telling of
All that had since occurred,
And proving to them totally
He'd been true to his word.

He'd wanted more than anything
To have the chance to stem
The bad thoughts they'd have had of him
And clear his name with them.

And now to think there was a chance
That they would never know
That he'd been forced away and that
He had been made to go.

They'd think he was a robber –
A notion they'd all share
Until their dying day – it was
Almost too much to bear.

They returned from whence they'd come –
Life went on as before.
And so the weeks passed by until
The summer came once more.

And Oliver's benefactors
Declared they'd now repair
Into the countryside and said
They had a cottage there.

And what a special time it was,
For now the sickly boy
Felt the peace, tranquillity
And very unique joy…

Of balmy air amongst green hills
And woods to wander through.
What an amazing contrast
To all the poor boy knew.

It was a happy, carefree time,
So peaceful and serene,
So different from the London streets,
All dingy, dark and mean.

A white-haired, ancient gentleman
Taught him how to write,
And he improved his reading too,
Then each and every night…

He'd curl up in his little bed
With no concern or fear
That anything remotely bad
Was likely to draw near.

And Rose and Mrs Maylie
Gave him such kindly looks,
And walked with him and talked about
All kinds of story books.

And so three months just glided by
And 'twould be true to say
That Oliver felt gratitude
On every single day.

And Rose and Mrs Maylie
For their true, kindly part,
Loved the boy – and Oliver,
Within his pure, young heart…

Felt such a deep attachment
That not a thing could dim;
And in return they felt a pride
And joy in loving him.

A CONFESSION TAKES PLACE

Now while all this is happening
We'll take the time to go
And make a little journey
To someone else we know.

I speak of Mr Bumble,
That proud, self-serving man
Who carries on in such a way
As only beadles can.

For they are most important
As we are all aware,
And everyone's respectful to
A beadle's steady stare.

Now beadle Bumble found himself
Very deeply drawn
To the matron of the Workhouse where
Poor Oliver was born.

Mrs Corney was her name,
And over cups of tea
Mr Bumble did his best —
And most affectionately…

To flirt with Mrs Corney;
And on one winter's day,
As they sat sipping steaming tea
He had these words to say.

'Are you hard-hearted ma'am?' he asked.
'Dear me,' the matron said,
'Whatever put a thought like that
Into your silly head?

'And what a question, I must say,
And from a single man.'
The beadle sipped his tea with ease,
For he now had a plan.

He finished off a slice of toast,
He whisked crumbs from his knee;
He wiped his lips with utmost care
And then deliberately…

He kissed the matron sitting there –
(So this then was his scheme)
The lady cried with frightened voice,
'Oh, bold sir – I shall scream.'

Bumble there made no reply
But slowly – without haste,
With dignity, he placed his arm
Around the matron's waist.

Now Mrs Corney was about
To scream as she had said,
But heavy knocking at the door
Made her just gasp instead.

And Bumble for his part – well he
Quickly then withdrew.
It was in truth his only course –
The proper thing to do.

And then a withered female put
Her head around the door;
She looked disheartened and her eyes
Were cast towards the floor.

She said, 'Old Sally's going fast,
It's very plain to see.'
The matron looked with flashing eyes,
'Well, what is that to me?

'For I can't keep her here alive.'
'No mistress,' came reply,
'She's far beyond the reach of help.'
She said this with a sigh.

'For I've seen many pass away,
From babes to great, strong men,
I know when deaths a-coming on,
For I can see it then.

'But she's a-troubled in her mind,
She's something she must tell.
It's almost like if it's not told
She thinks she'll go to hell.

'She says it's only for your ears,
Otherwise she's dumb.
I swear she won't die quietly,
Unless mistress, you come!'

At this remark the matron
Cursed and said, 'My, My!'
She muttered and then cursed those folk
Who wouldn't even die…

Without being of annoyance
Unto their betters – so
Although it was a nuisance
She thought she'd better go.

She asked the beadle Bumble
If he would kindly stay
And wait for her, with patience,
While she was thus away.

Now a timely small reminder
Would be in place and for
The fact we've met old Sally in
This narrative before.

For she was Sally Thingummy –
Now old and frail and worn –
And she was there upon the day
That Oliver was born.

She was the nurse who aided then
The surgeon at his birth,
The one who hit the bottle hard
For all that she was worth.

So Mrs Corney followed on
Into old Sally's room;
A doctor who was very young
Stood lurking in the gloom.

He greeted Mrs Corney,
Then said that he surmised
She wouldn't last an hour or two:
If so – he'd be surprised.

Mrs Corney then approached
As Sally lay quite still,
But then she shivered almost like
She had a frightful chill.

And then she lay there prone again
And Mrs Corney said,
'I'll not be waiting here for she
Is very nearly dead.'

She made to leave but as she did
A hollow voice cried out;
'Who's that?' came from the ailing crone –
It came as quite a shout.

'Hush, hush,' a woman tending said,
'Lie down – don't try to strive.'
The woman struggling then cried out,
'I'll not lie down alive…

'So let me speak before I die,
Come over now, d'ya hear.
Let me tell you what I know –
I'll whisper in your ear.'

Mrs Corney then drew close;
The dying woman said –
'Now listen, I once nursed a girl,
A-dying in this bed.

'A pretty creature who this life
Had very badly used,
For she came to this house alone,
Her feet all cut and bruised,

'And she gave birth then to a boy.
We laid him by her side.
What was the year? It matters not.
For then the poor girl died.

'Now what was I about to say?'
Her words came soft and slow.
Her face was flushed, her eyes stared out,
And then she cried, 'I know!

'I robbed her, so I did, it's true.
It was both bad and bold,
For when I stole it that poor girl
Still wasn't really cold.'

'Stole what?' the matron cried out loud,
Her voice an anxious shout.
'What did you steal for heaven's sake?
Come on I say – speak out.'

'The only thing the poor girl had –
And through her painful strife,
It could have kept her safe and fed;
It could have saved her life.

'For it was made of finest gold,
Yes, gold it was, I say.
It really could have saved the girl,
It could have saved the day.'

'You say 'twas gold,' the matron cried.
'Who was the mother? Speak.'
The dying woman spoke again,
Her voice was very weak.

'She was a suffering poor thing.
A wretched, lonely waif;
Afore she died she begged for me
To keep it close and safe.

'The little boy grew up in time
To look just like his mum.'
The dying wretch now seemed to be
Distraught and overcome.

'Poor, sweet girl – she was so young,'
She moaned now in a state.
The matron cried, 'Be quick, be quick,
Or it might be too late.

'Who was the boy? I need to know.
Tell if it's in your ken.'
'They called him Oliver,' she said.
'The gold I stole was…' – then

She sat bolt upright in the bed.
'Yes, yes,' the matron cried.
The woman fell back lifelessly
And in that second died.

'Stone dead,' a woman tending her
Was heard to softly say,
And Mrs Corney groaned, 'She died
And gave no clue away.'

So Sally Thingummy thus died,
But as she passed away,
She clung to Mrs Corney's gown –
She still had words to say;

But these words, they never came,
Her life had run its course,
So Mrs Corney pulled her hand
From off her gown with force.

And as she did she found the hand
Was tightly clasped around
A dirty scrap of paper which
Now fell on to the ground.

And when she looked to ascertain
Just what the paper was
Her heart leapt with excitement,
And this was just because…

She saw it was a ticket from
An old pawnbroker's shop,
And straightaway she then resolved
To go and make the swap.

She would redeem the item,
For from what Sally told
It could turn out to be the thing
Made out of finest gold.

~ ~ ~

And so upon the following day
Mrs Corney went
To the old pawnbroker's where
Some money was thus spent.

And in exchange the pawnbroker
Gave her a golden locket,
Which she examined carefully,
Then placed inside her pocket.

On getting back she took it out,
A shiny, lovely thing,
And it contained two locks of hair
And a gold wedding ring.

And there inscribed inside the lid,
'Agnes' was engraved.
She closed it with a soft, firm click,
And thought, 'This must be saved.

'I'll keep it safe, oh that I will.'
But as she spoke, it's true,
She didn't know the future or
What it would one day do.

A VISITOR

Now following the burglary
The Dodger came to say,
'We've got a visitor tonight.'
Old Fagin just said, 'Eh?'

'It's Toby Crackit,' Dodger breathed.
'Where is he?' Fagin said.
His eyes stared wildly as he shook
His mangy, withered head.

'I've put him in the room upstairs.'
So Fagin made his way
Up the creaking stairs to find
What Toby had to say.

'How are you Fagey?' Toby asked.
Old Fagin stared with ire
As Toby pulled his chair up to
A sad and sorry fire.

'Don't look at me like that, old man,
You know I cannot talk
'Bout business till I've had some food –
Get me a knife and fork.

'And bring some vittles right away.
I'm starving, that I am.'
So Dodger brought some bread and cheese –
Which Toby did then cram…

Into his mouth and then he said,
'First grub I've had in days.
I tell you Fagin, it ain't true
That stealing stuff still pays.'

Finally he'd had his fill.
When he could eat no more
He mixed a glass of spirits as
The Dodger closed the door.

'First and foremost Fagey,'
He held old Fagin's stare,
As Fagin interspersed, 'Yes. Yes!'
And sat down in a chair.

'How's old Bill been getting on?'
'What!' Fagin then screamed out.
'Where is the boy – and Bill – where's he?
What is this all about?'

Toby then spoke quietly.
'We all could now get jailed.'
He looked at Fagin nervously,
'Fagey – the crack – it failed.'

'I know. I know,' old Fagin said.
'What a stupid caper.
I saw it all, I read it here
In the daily paper.'

'They fired and hit the boy – we fled
Across the fields and then
They chased us with some fearsome dogs,
And there were loads of men.'

'The boy?' gasped Fagin in a state.
His eye began to twitch.
'We left the youngster,' Toby yelled,
'Lying in a ditch.

'And Bill and me we parted,
And left him lying, so
He could be still alive – or dead –
That's really all I know.'

Well Fagin shot right from his chair.
He uttered a loud yell.
He grabbed his hair – he wrung his hands,
And then he rushed pell-mell…

Out of the room – then out the house
Into the grimy street.
It seemed he had somewhere to go
Or someone he must meet.

A MYSTERIOUS CHARACTER APPEARS

Fraught Fagin scuttled down the street
In a disordered way;
His mind raced on from what he'd heard
Young Toby Crackit say.

He paused close by to bleak Snow Hill,
Then made his way along
A narrow, dismal alleyway
That had a dreadful pong.

Then on towards old Saffron Hill;
He saw a man he knew.
He asked, 'Who's up the road tonight?'
The man just sipped his brew.

And then he puffed upon his pipe,
And then he dourly said,
'At the Cripples?' – Fagin stopped
And nodded his old head.

'There's half a dozen there tonight.'
So Fagin hurried on.
The man called out but in a trice
Old Fagin's form was gone.

He'd disappeared into the night –
Then reached the Cripples pub.
A house of ill repute that served
Beer, spirits and rough grub.

Fagin entered quietly
Into the smoke filled room.
The lamps gave light to barely lift
The all pervading gloom.

And Fagin then spoke to a man.
'Will he be here tonight?'
'Do you mean Monks?' the man replied.
He looked to left and right.

'Hush, hush,' old Fagin breathed. 'Yes. Yes.'
The man looked at the door
As if to see if someone came.
'Oh he'll be here for sure.'

Fagin said, 'I cannot wait.
Tell him that I was here.
Tell him to come to see me soon.
Just tell him – is that clear?'

And then he hurried on his way
To make another call,
To see if Sikes was home yet – but
He'd not been home at all.

He spoke a while to Nancy
Then headed off once more,
And didn't rest till he approached
His own dark, shabby door.

As he prepared to open it
A stranger then drew near,
He came right up to Fagin and
He spoke into his ear.

'Where have you been then Fagin?
I've waited here two hours.'
These words were then accompanied with
Dark looks and heavy glowers.

'I've been about your business
As you'd expect I should.'
'What's the result?' the stranger asked.
'Nothing, my friend, that's good.'

'Well nothing bad, I really hope,'
The stranger roughly said.
Old Fagin stood transfixed and then
He slowly shook his head.

'Let's step inside,' the weird man rasped,
So Fagin let them in.
Into his dark and dismal home:
Into his den of sin.

'It's darker than a grave in here,'
The stranger said with fear.
'Make haste I say, I hate all this.
Quick – bring a candle near.'

Fagin did as he was bid,
Then they in whispers spoke,
And all the time the stranger stood
Enveloped in his cloak.

But Fagin knew the man all right,
For as the pair did speak,
He called him 'Mr Monks' – it was
The man he'd gone to seek.

But Monks was speaking now – he said,
'It was all badly planned.
You should have made a thief of him.
I just don't understand.

'You've done it with the other boys.
You could have got him caught,
And had him then deported, so
I really would have thought,

'It should have been quite easy,
To have him gone for life.
You could have saved a lot of time,
And mess and all – and strife!'

'What would you have me doing then?
And while he was our "lodger" –
I sent him out with Charley Bates
And with the artful Dodger.

'You know what happened then for he
Easily got caught,
But Nancy got him back although
'Twas not the end we sought.

'For she began to favour him.
Kind thoughts ran through her head.'
Monks stared back impatiently.
'Then throttle her,' he said.

They talked some more but time drew on,
And it was strange indeed,
The talk was all of Oliver,
His every word and deed.

And it was very obvious,
Monks wished the boy no good,
But finally he stretched and pulled
A black and shabby hood…

Across his head – 'twas time to go
For it was getting late.
And as Monks walked towards the door
His face was filled with hate.

Whatever could the reason be?
For as he clenched his fist
His mind was filled with awful thoughts
Of little Master Twist.

AN UNPLEASANT TIME FOR OLIVER

So let's return to Oliver,
There in the countryside,
Where Rose and Mrs Maylie,
With much maternal pride…

Shower love and fulsome happiness
Upon the ill-used boy,
And for his part, young Oliver
Found his new life a joy.

But now black clouds were gathering
And soon were close at hand,
For sweet, young Rose just felt so ill
That she could hardly stand.

She did her best to cover it,
Until on one bleak day,
She sat at the piano –
Her favourite song to play.

She did her best to form the tune
But then her fingers dropped
Onto the keys – she looked around
As all the music stopped.

And then her hands came to her face,
She was in much distress
As she gave way to flowing tears
She could not now repress.

'My child,' said Mrs Maylie,
'I vow I never saw
You get into a state like this –
I've not seen this before.'

Sick Rose spoke out and bravely
As she sat there, so still,
'I don't want to alarm you, but
I fear I'm very ill.'

And ill she was – no doubt at all –
In fact it's surely true,
To say she was more poorly than
Those present that day knew.

So to her bed, Rose was confined
And Mrs Maylie said,
'I fear misfortune Oliver
Will soon fall on our head.'

'What misfortune?' cried the boy.
She said, 'The heavy blow
That now has fallen on us and
Has laid my niece there low.

'I fear we may be losing her.'
Her eyes looked pained and wild.
'Oh God forbid!' cried Oliver.
'Amen to that, my child.'

The lady spoke with wringing hands.
Her sorry face just fell.
'Two hours ago,' cried Oliver,
'Our dear, sweet Rose looked well.'

But Mrs Maylie stood up straight,
For she would not give in.
She said, 'We must act urgently.'
Her mind was in a spin.

'The most important thing right now,
That we must surely do,
Is contact Dr Losberne
And get his expert view.

'I'll write a letter Oliver
That you can take to town.
You should be there and back before
The setting sun goes down.'

And so it was all quickly done,
And Oliver did doff
His woollen cap – then at a run
The troubled lad set off.

He ran down little byways
And through a tangled wood,
Across green open fields and past
Where old farm buildings stood.

He ran and ran till he reached town
And on arriving went
To the inn for he'd been told
They'd see the letter sent.

He paid the landlord who then gave
The letter to a man
Who jumped astride a big, brown horse
And off the fast steed ran.

Heading now for Chertsey
To bring help on its way,
And all the worried boy could do
Was clasp his hands and pray.

So Oliver now headed home.
He crossed the inn's old yard,
And as he went it's true to say
That he was praying hard.

He turned a corner hurriedly
Which caused him to provoke
An angry cry from a tall man
Wrapped in a long, black cloak.

For Oliver, by accident
Had stumbled right into
The man, for he had not espied
Him coming into view.

The man cried, 'What the devil's this?
You snivelling, young cur.'
Oliver politely said,
'I beg your pardon, sir.'

'Death,' the man then muttered,
Through squinting, dark eyelashes.
'Who'd have thought it. Here he is.
Grind the boy to ashes.'

'I'm sorry sir,' said Oliver.
'I hope you are not hurt.'
But all he got for a reply
Were words both hard and curt.

'Rot his bones,' the man cried out
In a frightful passion.
He ground his teeth then clenched them
In an awful fashion.

'If I had had the courage
To only say the word,
I could have done with him for sure
From everything I've heard.

'Black death upon your heart I say
And curses on your head.
What are you doing here you imp?'
The awful stranger said.

He shook his fists – he gnashed his teeth
As his foul words did flow,
And then he rushed to Oliver
As though he'd strike a blow.

But then he fell onto the ground.
It seemed he had been hit
By some strong, writhing, violent form
Of a great, foaming fit.

Oliver gazed upon him.
'He's mad,' he thought 'for sure.'
Then acting quite instinctively
He rushed to the inn door.

On entering he looked around,
His face ablaze – wide-eyed,
Then asked the folk if they would help
The wretched man outside.

They said they would, so Oliver
Then set off home again,
And left the man there writhing,
His face suffused with pain.

He took a final look at him
And though he didn't know,
It was someone who wished him ill,
A bitter, evil foe.

For the stranger lying there
Was no-one other than
The man who'd been with Fagin,
That dark and dreadful man.

Yes, it was Monks, who by sheer chance
Was passing by that day.
A man determined that he'd have
His selfish, evil way.

Oliver rushed homeward
And on arriving there,
He found that Rose was even worse,
Despite all loving care.

And things did not improve at all
Through the coming days,
And Dr Losberne, when he came
Explained, 'This dangerous phase…

'Could last a little while, but still
We mustn't give up hope.'
So somehow they all carried on
And found a way to cope.

And then one day fraught Oliver
Came home from being out
And found old Mrs Maylie –
Her face suffused with doubt…

Sitting in the parlour;
Whatever could be wrong?
For she had stayed at Rose's side
And been there all along.

Oliver now trembled
With fear he couldn't hide.
Whatever in this world had made
Her leave sick Rose's side?

He learned that Rose was sleeping
And if sweet Rose came round,
She then would go on living
And once again be sound.

So one way offered life and joy,
For which their hopes were high.
The other meant she'd never wake
And sadly she would die.

They sat for hours just waiting,
Afraid to speak a word.
The ticking of the clock was now
The only sound they heard.

But then they heard some footsteps,
They darted for the door;
Then Dr Losberne entered –
And from the look he wore…

'Twas really quite impossible
To easily discern
How their dearest Rose now fared –
But they would shortly learn.

'What of Rose?' the lady cried.
Her voice was strained and tense.
'Tell me at once, I cannot bear
This terrible suspense.

'Oh tell me now – in heaven's name.
Oh tell me now I pray.'
Dr Losberne quietly said,
'Be calm, dear ma'am, I say…

'You must compose yourself my dear.'
Mrs Maylie there was crying.
'Oh my sweet child – let me go in.
Oh my poor child is dying.'

'No, no,' cried Dr Losberne,
His face no longer glum,
'For Rose will live and bless us all
For many years to come.'

Mrs Maylie sank right down
Onto her creaking knees,
So grateful now that all was well –
That all her prayerful pleas…

Were answered in this moment:
She hugged the happy boy,
And both were filled with gratefulness
And overpowering joy.

And happily it all turned out
As Dr Losberne said.
Rose made a good recovery
And soon was out of bed.

A SHOCK FOR OLIVER

One lovely golden evening
That seemed of priceless worth,
When early shades of twilight
Had settled on the earth;

When shadows lengthened and the sun
Dipped in the western sky,
And when the glow of evening came
To bid the day goodbye,

We find young, earnest Oliver
With rapt and studied looks,
Sat at his workroom window
Intent upon his books.

Though it was hot and sultry
Oliver didn't shirk;
For quite some time that evening
He had been hard at work.

But then his head began to nod
And tiredness did creep
Across his weary, hard used eyes
Until he fell asleep.

There is a funny kind of sleep
That people sometimes find,
That holds the body prisoner
But still allows the mind…

To be aware of things about;
And though within sleep's womb –
Oliver was still aware
Of his own little room.

The table was before him.
His books were lying there –
The creeping plants outside were stirred
And by the twilight air.

And yet he was asleep he knew,
But then the scene – it changed.
The air became confined and close.
It all was rearranged.

He saw exactly where he was.
There was no room for error.
He was at Fagin's house again.
He felt a glow of terror.

There was the old man motionless
In his usual place,
All bent and old and withering
And hideous of face.

He whispered to another man
And though the light was dim
Oliver was certain that
He pointed straight at him.

'Hush, my dear,' he thought he heard
Old Fagin softly say.
'It is the boy, I'm sure enough —
And so now, come away.'

The man there with him then replied
And with an awful stare,
'Think you, I could mistake him then?
I'd know him anywhere.

'For if a crowd of clever ghosts
Took on the boy's same shape,
And if he stood amongst them all
Dressed in the same black cape…

'I'd point him out, I promise you.
There would be no mistake.'
The awful words made Oliver
Though dreaming, all but shake.

'If he was buried fifty feet,'
The man went on to rave,
'Deep in the ground and then I walked
Across his unmarked grave…

'I should still know for certain,
Without the slightest care
Of being wrong — I'd surely know
That he lay buried there.

'I told you it was him I saw.
I spotted him and knew
It could be no-one other and
You would know what to do.'

Dreadful hatred seemed to ooze
From every word he spoke,
And so with fright poor Oliver
Quite suddenly awoke.

Good heavens! – What was it
That sent his tingling blood
Racing to his pounding heart
In a torrential flood?

What was it stopped his power to move
And took his voice away?
What was it struck him down with fear
On that sweet, balmy day?

Why there – there at the window,
Close enough to touch.
Within such range to almost be
Within his horrid clutch.

His eyes were peering in the room
And with an awful stare.
Oliver looked in disbelief –
For Fagin stood right there!

And with him was a horrid man
With angry, scowling face.
The man looked evil, downright bad.
A scoundrel, foul and base.

And then he saw with certainty
And awful clinging dread,
It was the frightful man he'd seen
There at the inn – who'd said…

Such fearful, evil, crazy words.
Who'd tried to strike him too.
And who he was – scared Oliver
Had no idea or clue.

It was all in but an instant.
A flash that brightly shone,
A wicked glance, an evil stare
And then the pair were gone.

But they had recognised him
And he had seen them too,
And now they knew just where he was
Who knows what they might do.

The vision of the wicked pair
Chilled him to the bone,
Impressed upon his memory
As if 'twere carved in stone.

He stood transfixed and then he ran
And with an anguished yelp,
He called out to his loyal friends
A frantic cry for help.

When the inmates of the house
Heard Oliver's loud cry,
They quickly ran to ascertain –
To find the reason why…

The little boy seemed terrified;
Had he been hurt or not?
They ran to where the cry came from,
Right to the very spot…

And there they found scared Oliver;
His face was tense and pale,
And as he shook he raised his eyes
And moaned a mournful wail.

He pointed 'cross the meadow.
'Twas him. I saw him there.'
They led him very gently
And said, 'Rest in this chair.'

But the boy just pointed.
'Twas Fagin that I saw.
At my study window.
Yes him, I know for sure.

'And he was with the horrid man
I saw the other day,
When I was out – he spoke to me
In such a frightening way.

'And now they've run across the fields
But know that I am here.'
The little boy choked back his sobs
And trembled there in fear.

Giles and Dr Losberne
Who were both there as well
Thought – 'Oliver's being truthful
As far as we can tell.'

They hurried off to search the fields
But came back to confess
That they'd not seen a soul at all.
That they'd had no success.

O'er the coming days they asked
Around the countryside,
And in the nearby town as well –
Enquiring far and wide,

To ask if they'd been seen at all.
Had they been spotted there?
But no-one said they'd seen a trace
Of that dark, evil pair.

'Twas one more bad occurrence,
Unfortunate and rotten
For Oliver – but then in time
The whole thing was forgotten.

MR BUMBLE MEETS MONKS

We'll go in search of Bumble now
To see what he's been doing.
Well, while we've been away, the man
Has been most busy wooing.

For he's now gotten married
To Mrs Corney who
He's taken as his own dear wife –
But sometimes this he'd rue.

And like the job of threading
Fine cotton through a needle,
Life had become most hard because
He was no longer beadle.

He'd lost his grand position,
And now a married man
His world had been turned upside down,
As it so often can.

But one drab day whilst in a pub
A stranger spoke to him.
At first he thought it just by chance,
An idle, fickle whim.

But then the stranger turned the chat
Of which the thrusting gist,
Was to extract some word about
Our hero – Master Twist.

Or more specifically he wished
To know about his birth.
About the nurse who'd helped his mum;
That hag of dubious worth.

'Where is she?' he asked Bumble,
And Bumble then replied,
'No longer in employment for
Last winter – why she died.'

And then the cunning Bumble
Went on and archly said,
'There was a woman though who sat
By the old nurse's bed.

'She was right there before she died,
'And I believe she might
Have information given her
Upon that wintry night.

'For I've been told, before she passed
The old hag spoke to her.'
'How can I find her?' asked the man.
'Only through me, good sir.'

'When?' the stranger asked with haste.
'Tomorrow if you like.'
'That's good,' the stranger spoke again,
'When nine o'clock does strike.'

He pulled a scrap of paper
As he mumbled 'Yes'
To reaffirm the time and then
He scribbled an address.

It was a place located by
The dismal waterside.
He said, 'Keep all this secret –
Be certain that you hide…

'All details of our meeting,
I needn't stress to you,
That it is in your interest,
That this is what you do.'

And then they parted company;
As Bumble walked away
He looked down at the paper
To see what it would say.

He saw no name was written there
So quickly turned around
And caught the stranger up and touched
His arm but made no sound.

'Following me?' the stranger cried.
He spoke with angry ring.
Bumble, flustered, spoke out then,
'But just to ask one thing.

'What name am I to ask for?
That's all, good sir, I pray.'
The man just breathed the one word, 'Monks!'
And then he strode away.

The following night loud thunder raged,
The rain poured fiercely down,
As Bumble and his worthy wife
Walked through the darkened town.

Bumble checked his scrap of paper.
'This is the place,' he said.
He knocked – and right above him
They saw a man's dark head.

He called, 'Hang on, I'll be right down.'
And down he quickly came,
And it was Monks – oh yes 'twas him.
That man – the very same.

Once they were settled Monks then said,
'Now is this man here right?
You spoke with the old, dying hag
Upon that wretched night.

'She gave you information –
That's what I want to hear;
And he's your husband I believe.'
He said as he drew near.

'My husband is he?' she exclaimed.
'I thought so,' Monks replied.
''Twas obvious when you came in,
As you stood side by side.

'But I prefer it anyway,
For as you're man and wife
There is less chance of blabbing words –
Our secret running rife.'

He thrust his hand into his coat
And pulled a pile of cash.
'Here's five and twenty sovereigns then.'
He piled it in a stash.

'Now tell me everything you know.
And were you there alone?'
'Yes, no-one else was there,' she said.
'We spoke quite on our own.

'She told me of the frightened girl
Whose eyes were fixed and wild.
She said the lass had given birth
And to a healthy child.

'She said she'd stolen from the corpse
A locket on a chain.'
Monks's face contorted then
Into a mask of pain.

'Where is it now?' he grimly asked.
'Why here,' the woman said.
Monks grabbed the locket trembling.
His face was flushed bright red.

He opened it to find two locks
Of hair – and then the ring.
The woman said, 'Look take good heed
For there's another thing.

' "Agnes" is engraved within.'
'And is this all?' Monks cried.
She said, 'The hag was silent then,
And after that she died.'

Mr Bumble's face looked bleak;
He feared things might turn black.
He thought there was a chance that Monks
Might want his money back.

The locket was their bargaining tool,
They'd nothing else to sell.
He feared that Monks would think that as
They'd nothing else to tell…

His money was unwisely spent –
The deal would now be spurned,
And angrily he would insist
His money was returned.

But Monks seemed satisfied and then
He pushed his chair aside,
Which then revealed a wooden hatch
Which he threw open wide.

It was a trapdoor in the floor,
Right by old Bumble's chair.
'Look down,' Monks cried and both of them
Found they could then but stare…

Into the deep, dark abyss –
And heaving there below
Was a river rushing by
With dark and rapid flow.

Once there'd been a watermill
Upon this very site,
But now it was just foaming tide,
A-swirling round that night.

'If you flung a man down there,'
(Was this some kind of warning?)
'Where would he be?' said dreadful Monks,
'By this time next morning.'

 'Twelve miles down river,' Bumble said.
'Dragged by the current's motion.
And cut to pieces, likely too.'
He shuddered at the notion.

Monks placed the locket in a bag
With a leaden weight,
And with a face suffused with blood
And lips that curled in hate…

He dropped the bag into the hole;
It fell straight as a die.
Three doleful faces viewed its fall
And all three gave a sigh.

'There,' said Monks, 'Now if the sea
Gives up its dead – I'm told –
That it will keep forever though,
Its silver and its gold.'

'Of course,' said Bumble quietly.
'And now,' Monks gruffly said,
'I caution both of you to keep
A still tongue in your head.'

'Depend on it,' fat Bumble breathed,
And Monks was heard to say,
'I'm glad to hear it for if not
You could well rue the day.'

And then he showed them to the door,
Back to the cold, wet night,
And quickly then the evil Monks
Was soon lost to their sight.

NANCY HEARS A SECRET

Now as we know, around this time
Rose Maylie's health returned,
And so there was no further need
For all to be concerned.

And once she felt quite well again
She thought she'd travel down,
To spend a little holiday
In sprawling London town.

Her aunt would go along and yes
Young Oliver as well;
The city life with all its fun
Would surely then dispel…

The remnants of her illness;
Bring her to life again.
For from a spell in London town
There was so much to gain.

And so they set off joyfully
And on arriving there,
They found a comfy, small hotel
Close to a park's fresh air.

And now they're safely thus installed
Our story turns back to
Vile Fagin and the evil Monks
And what the pair now do.

They're meeting at old Fagin's place,
Surrounded by its gloom,
Locked deep in conversation
Within an upstairs room.

And while they talk in whispers
Nancy is outside;
Her ear is at the fastened door –
She listens there wide-eyed;

Appalled at what they're saying,
Behind the oaken door,
She makes her way back down again
Quietly once more.

And shortly afterwards she hears
Monks coming down the stairs,
It was apparent they'd now closed
Their secret, dark affairs.

He went away immediately,
Then Fagin came back down,
But as he looked at Nancy there
His face took on a frown.

'Why Nance,' old Fagin then exclaimed,
'You look extremely frail.
In fact you look quite horrible
And oh so very pale.

'What have you been a-doing Nance
To look so wan of face?'
'Nothing,' she replied, 'It's just
Being in this place.'

Fagin gave the girl some cash –
His face looked grim and black.
'Give this to Bill now he's returned.'
She sighed, 'I must get back.'

And when she reached the open street
She felt convulsed by fears.
She wrung her hands repeatedly
And then burst into tears.

But then she hurried homewards
And on arriving there
She gave the cash to Sikes and then
She sank into a chair.

Her mood was very bleak indeed
But she did all to keep
Her thoughts just to herself and so
Bill Sikes fell fast asleep.

He tossed and turned in fever.
The robber wasn't well,
For he had now withdrawn into
A hot and sickly shell.

Yet Nancy there would care for him
As but a woman can.
For all his faults, it was the case,
He'd always be 'her man'.

NANCY VISITS ROSE MAYLIE

Later on Bill Sikes awoke
And took a gulp of gin;
It seemed to give some small relief,
As trickling down his chin…

He took another gulp and said,
'It helps to ease my pain.'
Then said, 'You look just like a corpse
That's come to life again.

'What's got into you my girl?
What you got on yer mind?
I'll cut yer throat, oh that I will
If I should ever find…

'Yer up to somethin' dangerous.'
Then Nancy shrugged and said,
'Why do you look at me like that?'
And Sikes there shook his head.

'So what yer thinking of my girl?'
And as he spoke he spat.
'Of many things,' she said, 'But Bill
What are the odds in that?'

'Now come and sit aside me Nance.'
He pointed to a place
Right beside him – then he said,
'And put on yer own face.

'For if yer don't I'll alter it
In such a certain way
That you won't know it when you look –
And I mean what I say.'

She sat beside the fevered man,
He took her by the hand;
He gazed around abstractedly
And tried to understand…

Just where he was and who was she,
Then with no further peep,
He fell back on the pillow and
Was very soon asleep.

His arm fell down right by his side;
He lay there in a trance.
She whispered, 'I may be too late
But this is my best chance.

'The laudanum has knocked him out.
It's worked on him at last,
So I must be away right now,
For I must act – and fast!'

So hastily she dressed herself
In bonnet, shoes and shawl;
She looked across at Sikes who slept
And didn't move at all.

She half expected he might wake,
But saw no sign of motion
For he'd been knocked quite senseless by
The lethal sleeping potion.

But still she thought she might just feel
The robbers heavy hand
On her shoulder as he made
A vain attempt to stand.

But no – he lay there sleeping
And gave a drawn out snore,
And so she kissed him on the lips
Then slipped out through the door.

When she reached the street she heard
A watchman call the time.
'Twas half past nine and then far off
She heard a church clock chime.

She made her way from Spitalfields
To London's rich West End;
She tore along and elbowed folk
And some there did contend…

That she was mad because she rushed
With such compelling force;
Intent to never deviate
From her desperate course.

Finally she reached a spot
Quite close to lush Hyde Park.
The street was very handsome
And also very dark.

She stopped before a small hotel;
A lamp burnt at its door;
She checked the name and speedily,
To make quite certain sure…

This was the place she sought. It was –
And then a man appeared;
He looked at her disdainfully
As though he thought her weird.

'I've come to see a lady.'
He said, 'What lady pray?'
His words came out all scornfully
As if he'd like to say…

'Clear off – you've really no right here.'
But she spoke rapidly.
'Miss Maylie,' Nancy then replied.
'It's her I'd like to see.'

'What name am I to say?' he asked.
She said, 'Don't give a name.'
'What business then?' he said with scorn.
She sighed, 'It's all the same.

'But I must see the lady.'
The man just softly swore.
'Be off,' he said and forcefully,
And walked towards the door.

'Is there no-one here,' she cried,
'To help a wretch like me?'
Another man now heard her speak
And said quite pleasantly…

'Take her message up now Joe.
It can't do any harm.'
His words calmed Nancy for they were
Just like a healing balm.

'What's it to be?' the first man said.
'Tell her,' the fraught girl rasped,
'A woman asks to speak to her.
Alone!' then Nancy gasped.

Finally the man came back
And said, 'Now follow me.'
And thus it was that Nancy then
Saw who she'd come to see.

For there before her stood a girl,
So beautiful and slight,
And Nancy knew she was the one
She'd hoped to see that night.

She tossed her head back carelessly.
Rose thought she looked quite shady.
And Nancy said, 'It's very hard
To get to see you lady.

'If I had taken great offence
And gone off on my way,
As many in my place would do –
You would have rued the day.'

Rose replied, 'I'm sorry
If they were harsh to you,
But tell me please, how can I help?
Whatever can I do?'

Her tone was full of kindliness,
Dispelling Nancy's fears;
It took her strangely by surprise
And she burst into tears.

'Oh lady, lady!' she cried out,
Her hands clasped passionately,
'If there were more like you – I swear
There would be less like me.'

'Please sit down,' Rose then replied
In her kindly diction.
'I will be happy to give aid
If you are in affliction.'

Nancy said, 'Just let me stand –
For it is getting late,
And when you've heard me out – well then
Kind words may turn to hate.

'I've come tonight to speak about
Somebody we both know,
And I have much that I must say
Before I up and go.

'I'm here concerning Oliver.
Aye lady, yes it's true,
And though I know he's in good hands
And now quite safe with you…

'I've things that I must tell you of.'
Rose Maylie was all ears,
For this strange girl had set alight
A whole new stream of fears.

Nancy now composed herself
And she began to speak,
And Rose she listened avidly;
Her poor face looked quite bleak.

'Now Oliver will have told you
About his life before,
How he was forced by Fagin
To thieve and break the law.

'I've put my life at risk to come.'
Her voice was high and shrill.
'For on the night young Oliver
Went out in Pentonville…

''Twas me who dragged him off to be
At Fagin's place again.
'Twas me who caused his heartaches,
His torment and his pain.'

'You,' Rose Maylie then cried out.
'Aye lady – it was me.
I'm the one who just ignored
The poor boy's every plea.'

'What dreadful words you speak,' Rose cried.
And Nancy said through tears,
'Be grateful lady you were not
Beset through life with fears.

'That through your childhood you were blessed
With those who loved you so.
That cold and hunger were not things
You e'er had cause to know.

'The alley and the gutter,'
She then forlornly said
'Were my cradle as they'll be
My cheerless, cold deathbed.'

Rose clasped her hands, 'I pity you.'
And Nancy, in distress,
Said, 'Thank you for your goodness –
Oh thank you and God Bless.

'But I must speak and tell you
I have so much to fear,
For there are those who'd murder me
If they knew I was here.

'But to the question I must ask,
Now do you know a man
By the name of Monks – recall
Good lady if you can?'

'I've never heard the name,' said Rose.
Nancy's eyes shone bright.
'I hid while he was talking
To Fagin, one dark night.

''Twas after you took Oliver
Into your house – you know –
Following the robbery,
So quite some time ago.

'Monks was telling Fagin
That he'd seen the lad,
With two of Fagin's boys when they
Were acting very bad.

'He saw them stealing from a man.
They took his handkerchief.
That's when Oliver was taken –
Arrested as a thief.

'"Twas on that day we lost him first.'
Her voice was a low groan.
'And Monks told wretched Fagin
That he had quickly known…

'It was the very boy he sought.'
And then she gave a sigh.
'He had searched for him although
I couldn't make out why.

'But he struck a deal with Fagin
Which was beyond belief.
He wanted Oliver to be
Just turned into a thief.

'He said he'd pay old Fagin
Once the deed was done.'
'For what purpose?' asked sweet Rose.
Her rapt attention won.

Nancy said, 'At just that point
I thought they were aware
Of my presence – so I went –
It gave me quite a scare.

'I saw no more of Mr Monks.
No – not another sight,
That was, dear lady, till I saw
The man again, last night.

'He came and once again they climbed
Up to the upstairs room,
And once again I followed them
And stood there in the gloom.

'The first thing that I heard bad Monks
Say to old Fagin there,
When both were sure they were alone,
(They'd taken all due care)

'Were words that sent an awful chill
Running through my frame.
I heard them speak about the boy –
Heard Oliver's sweet name.

'They said he was in London
And said exactly where,
And so I knew that Oliver
Had good cause to beware.

'Monks said, "And so the only proof
Of his identity
Lies at the river's bottom –
That's where it's best to be.

' "And the hag who stole the proof
Is rotting in her grave."
And Fagin then just laughed out loud,
And so did Monks – the knave.

'And then Monks said he'd rather
Have had it t'other way.
Have seen the boy in every jail,
And then went on to say…

'He had the little devil's cash.
'Twas in his grasp right now,
And so it made no difference,
He had it anyhow.

'Oliver's inheritance
Would stay with him he said.
'Twould never reach its rightful heir
Although his dad was dead.'

'What does this mean?' Rose then cried out.
'The truth,' Nancy replied.
'Is that Monks said he'd sooner
The boy had somehow died.

'He said if he could get away
With killing him, he would,
For even now he'd cause him harm,
If he thought that he could.

'He told old Fagin forcefully,
"I swear upon my mother,
You've never laid out snares as I
Would lay out for my brother." '

'His brother!!' Rose exclaimed aghast,
No longer so serene.
'You say he spoke in earnest.
Whatever does this mean?

'How can I use this confidence
And how can I help you?'
Nancy shrugged and sadly said,
'There's nothing you can do.

'And I must go back now – I must,
There's one I cannot leave.'
She wiped away a wretched tear
With her old tattered sleeve.

Sweet Rose cried out, 'I'll save you
From all your awful strife,
Let me help you find a way
To live a better life.'

'Dear sweet lady,' said the girl,
'You are the very first
To bless me with such words as these,
For normally I'm cursed.

'There really is no hope for me,
Today or then tomorrow,
If I had heard them years ago
I could have seen less sorrow.

'But it is much too late for me.'
She now seemed out of breath.
'I cannot leave him now – I can't.
I could not cause his death.'

'It never is too late,' Rose said.
'It is,' the girl cried out.
The way she spoke just clearly showed
That she was in no doubt.

'How can I use this confidence?'
Rose asked, 'What should I do?'
And Nancy said, 'You must have friends
Who'll give advice to you.

'Perhaps a kindly gentleman.'
Rose nodded as she spoke.
She thought it all so awful – wished
It was some kind of joke.

'But how can I get hold of you?'
Rose asked the frightened girl.
Nancy stood there thinking.
Her mind was in a whirl.

She shook with deep emotion,
It seemed to overpower.
And then with heaving sighs she said,
'Around the midnight hour…

'On every Sunday evening,
I faithfully will strive
To walk on London Bridge – that is
If I am still alive.'

'Stay a moment more,' said Rose.
'Can I not change your mind?
Stay with me – do not return,
Together we can find…

'A better life for you to live;
Oh please, I beg and pray
That you will take this chance with me
To find a better way.'

'God bless you lady,' Nancy cried,
'But there's no helping me.
It would be better if I died
For it would set me free.'

'Take some money,' Rose cried out.
But Nancy just said, 'No!'
And then she made it very clear
That it was time to go.

And so the desperate creature,
With nothing more to say,
Sobbing out as though she'd die –
Turned round to go away.

She left Rose Maylie sitting there
Not knowing what to do,
Overpowered and mortified
By this interview.

She sank into a soft, green chair,
Quite at her last resorts,
And did her very best to calm
Her wild and wandering thoughts.

OLIVER IS REACQUAINTED WITH AN OLD FRIEND

Shortly after these events
Rose sat alone one day
When Oliver came rushing in;
She said, 'Now tell me pray…

'What makes you look so flurried?
My dear – please tell me now.'
The young boy caught his breath and said,
'I almost don't know how.

'I feel as if I just might choke,
To think that I should see
That very special person –
He was so close to me;

'And now you'll know I spoke the truth.'
Rose said, 'I knew you had.'
But then she looked with great concern
At the excited lad.

'What is this all about?' she asked.
'Tell me of whom you speak?'
Oliver stood shaking and
He was so red of cheek.

He said, 'I've seen the gentleman
Who was so good to me.
I've just seen Mr Brownlow.'
'Where?' she asked eagerly.

'He was alighting from a coach.
I couldn't speak to him
Because I trembled massively
In every single limb.

'But Giles went to the house and asked,
For I just couldn't dare,
If Mr Brownlow did indeed
Truly live right there.

'They said he did and look I've got
A scrap of paper here.
It's where he lives – I'm going there.
Oh dear, oh dear, oh dear.'

Rose took the piece of paper from
Flushed Oliver's small hand;
She saw the house was very close,
Just somewhere off the Strand.

'Quick,' she said, 'Go fetch a coach,
We'll go there right away,
There's not a moment now to lose,
There must be no delay.'

And so within five minutes
They hurried off to meet
Mr Brownlow – by the Strand,
Right there in Craven Street.

When they arrived Rose knocked the door,
She went first on her own;
She left excited Oliver,
In the coach alone.

A servant showed her up to where
Good Brownlow sat that day.
He rose on seeing her and said,
'Be seated – please – I pray.'

She said, 'You're Mr Brownlow.'
He said, 'The very same,
And this is Mr Grimwig.'
And then she gave her name.

'And now,' she said, 'I must explain
My purpose being here –
I've come to speak of someone
Whom you once held most dear.

'He is a much loved friend of mine
And I am very sure
You'd like to hear about him and
Learn of his life once more.'

'Indeed!' said Mr Brownlow,
'You make a handsome claim.
Respectfully Miss Maylie
May I now ask his name?'

Rose clenched her hand quite nervously
And formed it in a fist.
She said, 'You knew him at the time
As little Master Twist.

'His first name was just Oliver – '
'Oliver Twist,' he cried.
And Mr Grimwig stared ahead,
And then he coughed and sighed.

But Mr Brownlow drew his chair
Up close to nervous Rose,
And said he would appreciate
If she would now disclose…

All she knew of Oliver.
He hoped she truly could
Change his views about the boy
And prove that he was good.

And so Rose told him everything,
And when the girl was done,
Mr Brownlow sighed and said,
'It's quite a tale you've spun.

'And this brings me great happiness –
And such relief right through,
But my dear – why did he not
Come along with you?'

Rose said, 'He's waiting in a coach –
Why at this very door.'
'At this door!' cried Brownlow.
He didn't wait for more.

He got up from his chair in haste,
He hurried from the room.
In fact it would be fair to say
He went off at a zoom.

Down the stairs he went and then
Up the coach steps there.
This was the answer to his dreams
And every fervent prayer.

Oh to be reunited
In such a happy way,
It really was incredible,
Oh such a happy day.

The joyful pair returned then to
The upstairs parlour where
Sweet Rose sat waiting patiently,
And also in his chair…

Sat Mr Grimwig, who in truth,
Had nothing bad to say,
And he received young Oliver
In a most gracious way.

Then Mr Brownlow rang the bell
And said, 'There's someone too
Who will be overjoyed to come
And say hello to you.'

Then Mrs Bedwin entered,
And when she saw the boy,
Her kindly heart just overflowed
With overpowering joy.

'God be good to me,' she cried.
And how her face did crack
Into the broadest smile – she said,
'I knew that he'd come back.'

'My dear old nurse,' cried Oliver,
And she then for her part
Just talked as she unloaded
The love within her heart.

'How well he looks – where have you been?
And how well dressed you are.
The same sweet face – the same soft eye.'
Nothing could now mar…

The dear old lady's pleasure.
'Oh what a lovely smile.
Where have you been a-hiding
All this long, long while?'

And so this great reunion
Brought happiness to all,
It really was a wonderful
Event to thus befall.

Now Mr Brownlow took good Rose
Into another room,
And once they were well settled
He asked her to resume…

In telling him just everything.
She did it once again,
She tried to tell him all of it,
She really wracked her brain.

When she was done – wise Brownlow said
'There's but one thing to do,
And that's to find this Monks and then –
By the time I'm through…

'We'll know of the boy's parentage
And also make some sense
Of Monks's talk about the lad,
And then we may commence…

'To find out what the boy is due,
For, from what you've said,
He's due inheritance and from
His father who is dead.'

'How can we ever find him?'
Rose asked with great concern.
And Mr Brownlow answered her,
His face now looking stern.

'We'll get to him through Nancy.
You said each Sunday night,
She vowed she'd be at London Bridge;
Well I think I just might…

'Arrange to go and meet her,
She'll surely tell us how
We can get to Monks,' and then
He wiped his furrowed brow…

And said – 'I'll get the truth for sure.
I'll drag it from this man.'
She said,' You think you're able?'
He said, 'I think I can.

'It's Tuesday now – but I will go
This coming Sunday night
And meet with Nancy and with luck
It all will turn out right.'

A MEETING ON LONDON BRIDGE

The church bell chimed three quarters past
Eleven of the clock;
A woman in a tattered coat –
Drawn tightly round her frock…

Advanced across old London Bridge,
With swift steps o'er the ground,
And as she walked she earnestly
Looked nervously around.

And then a little way behind
Another figure slunk,
And if the woman stopped, this man
With lightning speed then shrunk…

Into the deepest shadows
That he could quickly find;
He kept well out of sight, as he
Followed from behind.

The night was very, very dark;
Few people were about.
A mist hung on the river –
There really was no doubt…

'Twas not a night to be abroad,
All cold and black and grim,
With scarce a light and thus the world
Looked eerie, damp and dim.

So what was all of this about?
Who was the woman there,
Who seemed to be so burdened down
With every kind of care?

Well it was Nancy, who had said,
On every Sunday night,
She'd walk along old London Bridge,
In case Rose Maylie might…

Have cause to get in touch with her –
So this is what she did.
And who was it who followed her,
And when she stopped – then hid?

Well it was one of Fagin's gang,
Who had been told to tail
And keep an eye on Nancy,
And find out – without fail…

What she was up and doing,
For there had been a change
In how young Nancy acted;
Her manner had been strange.

And Fagin – he had noticed
That something was amiss.
He'd said, 'I really do not like
The manner of that miss.

'She's up to something – that's for sure,
So I am of the view,
To have her followed all the time
Would be the thing to do.'

So Nancy now paced to and fro
Watched by the hidden male
Who'd followed her across the town;
Old Fagin's secret tail.

And then the heavy bells of great
St. Paul's – across the way,
Tolled out the cold, remorseless death
Of yet another day.

For midnight had now fallen –
With no trace of pity –
On everything contained within
The crowded, sprawling city.

Upon the palace and the jail,
On those that were defiled,
Upon the corpse's rigid face,
Upon the sleeping child.

It had fallen on the desolate,
On those both short and tall,
On happy folk and those borne down.
Midnight fell on them all.

The hour had only just been struck
When a young lady stepped
From a hackney carriage which
Had seemingly just crept…

Up to the bridge, and quietly –
Had stopped on that dark night,
To let the lady and a man
Both gingerly alight.

The gentleman was grey of hair
And rigid in his bearing,
And from his certain manner and
The clothes that he was wearing…

It told he had authority;
So it's of no surprise,
The man was that good gentleman,
So kindly and so wise…

We know as Mr Brownlow,
And with him that cold night,
Was sweet Rose Maylie who had come
To try to set things right.

And so the kind, unselfish pair
Made their way along
Old London Bridge with hopeful hearts
They'd right an awful wrong.

They'd hardly walked a step or two
When Nancy saw them there;
She started then immediately –
With fixed and frightened stare…

To make her way towards them
And when they met she said,
'Not here – for I'm afraid to speak,'
And then she bowed her head.

It seemed she was intent to hide
Her features, just in case
Somebody who was passing by
Might recognise her face.

'No, come out of the public road.'
She didn't want to squander
This chance to speak and so she said,
'Down the steps there yonder.'

She pointed with her hand towards
Some steps that led right down
To the River Thames there on
The Surrey side of town.

The steps were in three flights – they turned
At angles as they went.
And thus for someone hiding there
They were quite heaven sent.

It made it very easy for
Someone to hide away
And listen to what furtive folk
Had gone down there to say.

Old Fagin's lad had guessed what they
Now proposed to do,
And so he darted down the stairs
And hid there out of view.

He was now in a perfect place
To hear their every word,
And so could tell old Fagin
Just all that had occurred.

He lurked there listening and then
He heard a firm rebuff.
'We'll not go any further down.
This is quite far enough.'

'Twas Mr Brownlow speaking.
He said, 'We'll humour you.
Why could we not speak up above
To do what we need do?'

'To humour me!' cried Nancy.
'To humour me, you say.
I told you I was scared to speak
There in the public way.

'I have such awful fear and dread
Upon my soul tonight
That if I am to speak to you
It must be out of sight.'

'A fear of what?' good Brownlow asked.
'I scarcely know,' she said.
'Awful thoughts – I see myself
In pools of blood – and dead.'

'Speak kindly to her,' sweet Rose begged.
And Nancy's passion grew.
She cried, 'Oh lady, why aren't folk
As kind and sweet as you?

'Those who claim they're God's own folk
Don't ever seem to see
How they could help poor wretches,
Just like the likes of me.'

'Who are you scared of?' Brownlow asked.
Nancy turned away.
'Oh, my Bill,' she said, 'but I
Think I am safe today.'

Brownlow nodded seriously,
Then said, 'I'll tell you now,
We intend to seek this Monks,
And this I also vow

'We do intend to get from him,
In any way we can,
The secret that is carried by
This dark and dangerous man.

'And if we fail to find him,
Well then we'll want you to
Give Fagin to us.' She cried out,
'Why that I'll never do.'

'You will not do this?' Brownlow asked.
'Never!' said the girl.
'Tell me why?' he challenged her;
She said, all in a whirl…

'Although he's led an awful life,
In truth – I have as well;
And all of us are surely soon
On our way to hell,

'But we've kept a course together;
I'll not turn on those who might
Have turned on me but didn't –
And though it isn't right…

'I'll stick with them through thick and thin.
The lady understands.'
Then Brownlow said, 'Well do one thing,
Put Monks into my hands.

'And once we've got the truth from him,
Well there we'll let things lay.
We'll stand aside – they'll all go free.
So now then – what d'you say?'

'Have I the lady's promise?'
Asked Nancy, on the edge.
She shook as Rose replied and vowed,
'You have my faithful pledge.'

'So Monks will never, ever know
How you know what you do?'
Brownlow answered Nancy then,
'This I promise you.'

She looked into his open face,
And she could plainly see
That every feature there displayed
Just spoke of honesty.

Nancy said, 'I've been a liar
All my whole life through.
Ever since I was a child –
And lived with liars too.

'But I shall take your given word.'
Then in a voice so low
She told them every single thing
That she had come to know.

She told them where Monks frequented,
The place he might be found.
And all the time she spoke she looked
Nervously around.

And then she told them how he looked.
'He's tall and strongly made.
He has a lurking style of walk
And seems to hug the shade.

'And constantly he turns to look
One way – then another,
As if he thinks he's followed by
Some dark and furtive other.

'His eyes are sunk into his head,
His face is dark – his hair
Is black as night and in his eyes
Is the most dismal stare.

'And though in his mid twenties,
He's a withered laggard;
His features are all pale and wan,
Worn down and very haggard.

'His lips are oft disfigured
By deep marks from his teeth,
For he has awful fits that are
Quite beyond belief.

'Sometimes he even bites his hands,
And there upon his throat,
Which usually is well concealed
Underneath his coat…'

'Is a mark just like a burn,'
Cried Brownlow – then 'O lor.'
And Nancy said, 'You know him then.
You've met somewhere before?'

'I think we have,' Brownlow replied.
'But not known by this name,
But then some folk are so alike;
He may not be the same.'

He moved close to the spot we know
The watching spy to be,
And so the spy there heard him say,
'For sure – it must be he!'

Then Mr Brownlow moved back to
The spot where he had stood,
He felt he must assist the girl,
He really felt he should.

He said, 'You've helped us very much
And so I'd like to do
Something to make things better –
To bring some help to you.

'What can I do to give you aid?'
'Nothing,' came reply.
'There's nothing can be done to help.'
She said this with a sigh.

'For I'm now chained to this my life,
And though I hate it so,
It is too late for me and it's
The only life I know.'

Mr Brownlow offered her
Escape from all the strife.
He offered her the means to start
A new and better life.

He said, 'Either here in England,
Or maybe overseas.'
But Nancy's ears were deaf to all
His fervent, heartfelt pleas.

Then Nancy cried, 'I must go home.'
'Home?' Rose sadly said.
And Nancy sighed, 'Yes lady,
And to a place I dread;

'But truly it's the only home
That I have ever known,
Built with the trials of my whole life.'
She said this with a moan.

'So let us part and if I've been
Of service to you two,
Well then just leave me be for this
Is all I ask of you.'

'It's useless,' Mr Brownlow said.
'We mustn't keep you here,
We compromise your safety
By holding you, my dear.'

'Yes, yes,' urged Nancy. 'Yes you do.'
Then Rose cried out with force,
'What will become of you? You're set
Upon a dismal course.'

'Now look before you lady.'
Nancy gave no quarter.
She'd not be swayed and softly said,
'Look at that dark water.

'How many times have you both heard
Of one the likes of me,
Who springs into the raging tide
To be set quickly free?

'Who leaves no living thing behind
To bewail their going.
It may be years, it may be months,
I have no way of knowing…

'But I shall come to that I'm sure
On some dark, future day.'
Poor Rose sobbed loudly and then said,
'Do not speak thus I pray.'

'Oh it will never reach your ears,
And God forbid it should.'
Nancy spoke as only one
In her position could.

'And now goodnight,' she firmly said,
But how her voice did quake.
'Please take this purse,' Rose cried out then.
'Oh take it for my sake.'

'No, no,' cried Nancy, 'I will not.
I did this not for gain,
And yet – give me a thing you've worn,
Just something very plain.

'A handkerchief or maybe gloves,
Anything will do,
Just so that lady, I can think
It once belonged to you.'

Rose did as she requested
Then Nancy rushed away
As if some awful happening
Would come to pass that day.

They heard her footsteps dying out,
Then climbed the steps to see
That Nancy stood there some way off;
Said Brownlow, 'Let her be.'

And so they turned and walked away,
And as they disappeared,
The girl sank down upon a step,
And everything she feared…

Welled up inside her breast and then
She shed such bitter tears
Which totally encompassed
Her lifetime's tragic fears.

And then she rose and tottered off,
With tear-stained, worn-down face,
And then the hidden spy emerged
From in his hiding place.

He looked around to ascertain
That he was all alone,
And when he was quite sure that he
Was truly on his own…

He set off in the shadows for
A place we've come to know.
He headed for old Fagin's house
As fast as he could go.

FATAL CONSEQUENCES

It was the middle of the night,
That cold and lifeless time,
Which so appeals to those who make
Their living out of crime.

And so we go to Fagin's den.
It's where our scene is cast.
And there sits Fagin waiting,
And then he mouthed, 'At last.'

He'd heard the bell a-ringing.
Someone was at the door.
He crept upstairs to open it,
And when he did he saw…

A man all muffled to his chin,
A bundle in one arm,
And by his look he seemed to be
Intent on doing harm.

So brutal in appearance,
His manner angry too,
He was quite clearly someone
That skulking Fagin knew.

He bade the man, 'Come in at once.'
Then by a dim, small light
Bill Sikes's face was lit – 'twas he
Who came on this bleak night.

When they were settled back downstairs
The dreadful, evil man
Pointed to his bundle there,
And said, 'Do what you can…

'To get the best price possible,
For it's been hard enough
To get my hands upon that stash
Of fine and lovely stuff.'

Fagin locked the bundle in
A cupboard by his side;
He watched Bill Sikes and as he did
Fagin was wide eyed.

His lips were quivering violently
Just like a frightened rat.
Sikes said, 'Why do you look at me
In such a way – like that?'

Then Fagin raised his finger,
His face borne down and wan,
He tried to speak but found that now
His power of speech was gone.

'Damn me,' Sikes cried, 'the man's gone mad.'
His face looked mean and black.
'No, no,' cried Fagin – having now –
Just then, got his voice back.

'Oh so yer 'aven't,' Sikes exclaimed.
'Well that's a piece of luck.
But what's got into you to make
Yer nervous and dumbstruck?'

Fagin drew his chair in close,
He said, 'Now Bill, d'ya see
I've got a thing to tell that will
Make you much worse than me.'

'What?' the robber said – he had
A disbelieving air.
'Tell away, look sharp for Nance
Will think I'm lost somewhere.'

'Lost!' cried Fagin. 'That's a joke,
For when you know the score,
You'll think she's settled that herself,
Yes sorted that for sure.'

Sikes looked most perplexed indeed.
He didn't understand.
He grabbed old Fagin's collar in
His coarse, enormous hand.

'Speak will yer,' he cried angrily,
His face a mask like death,
'And if yer don't, I'll make it so
It's 'cos of want of breath.

'Open yer old mangy mouth.
Say what you've got to say.
Out with it yer thundering cur,
Let's have no more delay.'

Fagin said, 'If that young lad' —
He looked towards his spy —
'Was to peach upon us all,
How should he pay — and why?

'If he crept out in dead of night
Seeking out fine folk,
Just for this very purpose — well,
It wouldn't be a joke.

'If he described us all and then
Said where we could be found,
D'you hear me Bill?' he cried aloud;
He made a shrieking sound.

'Suppose he did all this — what then?'
'What then?' foul Sikes replied.
'Well he'd be well advised to find
Some place where he could hide.

'For I would grind his skull beneath
My iron heel,' he said.
'Into as many grains as there
Are hairs upon his head.'

'And what if it were me — what then?'
Cried Fagin in a yell.
Sikes clenched his teeth and shouted out,
'I'd smash your head as well.'

'You would?' said Fagin archly.
'Just try me,' Sikes replied.
'If it were Charley, Dodger…'
'I don't care who,' Sikes cried.

'It could be anybody,
No matter what their name.
I tell you Fagin — if they peached
I'd serve them just the same.'

Fagin called the spy across,
The lad let out a yawn.
'He's tired of watching,' Fagin said.
'The girl — from dusk to dawn.'

'Wot d'yer mean?' Sikes tersely asked.
And Fagin told the lad.
'Tell me again for him to hear,
About the night you've had.'

'Tell yer what?' the boy replied.
''Bout Nancy,' Fagin said.
'You followed her to London Bridge
When folk should be abed.

'She met some folk at midnight.'
'She did,' the boy replied.
And then he told them everything –
And Sikes there at his side…

Went every shade of brightest red,
His eyes flashed, he looked wild,
The more the lad kept speaking –
The more Bill Sikes got riled.

Finally he cried, 'Hell's fire!
Let me get out of here.'
And in that moment it was plain
The girl had much to fear.

'Bill, Bill,' old Fagin called out then,
'A word, only a word.'
But Sikes was in no mood to stop.
It seemed he hadn't heard.

'Let me out,' he cried, but still
Old Fagin called his name.
'Don't speak to me – it isn't safe.
I say – this is no game.'

But Fagin kept on trying.
'Just hear a word,' he said.
Sikes stopped for just a moment then
And slightly turned his head.

'Well?' he breathed. – When Fagin spoke
His voice was high and shrill.
'You won't be – well – you won't be too…
You won't be violent Bill.'

A candle gave a flickering light –
Enough for each to see
The others mangled, tangled face,
And see it easily.

Their eyes met for a moment,
Their faces filled with ire,
And each could see the others eyes
Were alight – on fire.

Sikes made no reply but now
He just pulled back the door
And dashed off down the silent street
And then was seen no more.

Without one pause – without a look
To left or to the right,
He strode on now in silence in
The night-time's dingy light.

A savage resolution
Gripped his very being.
He strode along remorselessly,
His angry eyes unseeing.

His teeth were clenched and tightly,
The thief held to his course;
There was no doubt, his mood would soon
Translate into brute force.

He muttered not a single word;
Fraught – tense – right to his core,
His every muscle strained until
He reached his own front door.

He turned the key most softly,
Strode quickly up the stairs,
Went to their room and locked it;
Piled tables and some chairs…

Against the door to make quite sure
No-one could come inside,
Then strode across the room and drew
The bed drapes open wide.

Nancy lay there on the bed.
Asleep – and so it took
A moment to come fully round,
And then with startled look…

She saw Bill Sikes above her.
'Get up,' he roughly said.
'It's you,' she said with pleasure.
He stared down at the bed.

'It is,' he said. 'Now get on up!'
A candle was there burning.
He flung it then into the grate,
Emotions all a-churning.

Nancy rose to draw the curtains.
He yelled, 'I'm telling you,
Leave it for there's light enough
To do what I must do.'

'Bill,' – the girl was speaking in
The low voice of alarm,
For now she had begun to fear
He'd come to do her harm.

'Why do you look at me like that?'
And for a moment then
The robber sat regarding her –
The evilest of men.

His nostrils then dilated,
His breathing heavy too.
His face was turning very red,
His lips were turning blue.

And then he grabbed her by the throat
And placed his other hand
Upon her mouth – and Nancy then
Found it hard to stand.

She cried, 'Bill, Bill' – and struggled
In fear she was to die.
'Let me speak – what have I done?
I won't scream out or cry.'

'Yer know just what yer've done,' he yelled.
'She-devil – every word
You spoke tonight on London Bridge,
Well it was overheard.

'Old Fagin had yer watched me girl.'
His words cut like a knife.
'Bill, Bill – for love of heaven.
Dear Bill, please spare my life.

'You cannot have the heart – oh Bill –
To kill me. Do not do
What you will live to then regret;
Think – all I've done for you.

'Don't act in haste for mercy's sake,
Give yourself the time
To think about just what you do
And save yourself this crime.

'Bill, Bill, for dear God's sake – oh Bill.'
Her words came in a flood.
'I've always stayed so true – Bill stop
Before you spill my blood.'

Sikes struggled with her violently,
Her arms flailed at him so.
She cried, 'The gentleman tonight
Told of a place to go.

'A foreign land where I'd be safe,
He said he'd help me flee
So I could ask the gentleman
If he could try to see…

'If he could help the pair of us
To get away from this.
To help us leave this life behind.
There's nothing here we'd miss.

'Let me see them both again
And beg them on my knees,
I'm sure they'll help us when they hear
My true and heartfelt pleas.

'It never is too late, dear Bill.
We only need some time.'
But Sikes was now intent upon
His dastardly, foul crime.

He freed one arm and firmly grasped
His pistol – but then thought,
If he fired it, it might mean
He'd easily be caught.

'Twould mean he'd be detected.
'Twould surely be the case.
And so he smashed the gun with force
Into her upturned face.

She staggered back now blinded
With blood that spurted out
From a gash upon her head –
But still she didn't shout.

She raised herself onto her knees,
Ignoring the foul thief,
And from her heaving bosom took
A crisp, white handkerchief.

It was Rose Maylie's treasured gift
She clasped in folded hands,
With tear filled eyes and with her hair
Falling down in strands…

She raised her bloodied, beaten face –
She held the hanky high –
And breathed a prayer for mercy, then
Gasped out a soulful sigh.

It was a ghastly thing to thus
So terribly befall.
The brutal Sikes just staggered back
Against the grimy wall.

He shut out then this grizzly scene
With his rough, upturned hand.
For even he found such a sight
A mite too much to stand.

He grabbed a club from by the wall,
His face a fearful frown,
And with a mighty, swinging blow
He struck poor Nancy down.

THE FLIGHT OF SIKES

Of all the evil deeds with which
London has been cursed,
The murder of poor Nancy
Must surely be the worst.

Of all the acts committed
In darkness of the night,
Of all the awful crimes of hate,
Of malice and of spite…

Of all the deeds thus set afire
By wickedness's fuel,
This was without a trace of doubt
The foulest and most cruel.

The sun – the bright and warming sun
That brings not light alone,
But sheds new life and hope upon
The very smallest stone…

Now burst upon the city streets,
To light the city's story;
It filled the crowded alleyways
With clear and radiant glory.

Through costly-coloured glass it shone,
Through paper-mended pane,
Across the great cathedral dome –
On each foul smelling drain.

On every rotten crevice,
It shed its equal ray.
It lighted up the room wherein
The murdered woman lay.

He tried to shut the sunshine out,
But now his dreadful sin
Was all lit up and beams of warmth
Came boldly streaming in.

This sight that had been ghastly
In dullness of the night,
Was now increased tenfold there in
The brilliant morning light.

He hadn't stirred – he'd been afraid,
And totally unmanned,
And then he'd heard a feeble moan
And motion of the hand.

And as a terror gripped him
Wrapped in such hate and pain,
He'd taken up his lethal club
And struck and struck again.

Once he threw a rug across
The body lying there,
But then he'd fancy that her eyes –
With such an awful stare…

Were glaring out towards him,
So pulled the rug again
And saw her lying there and in
An awful, blood red stain.

There was the body – silent.
Mere flesh and blood, no more.
But oh such flesh and oh such blood,
Just lying on the floor.

He struck a light and made a fire
And poked the club into
The leaping flames and then he saw
Some human hair there too.

It blazed and shrunk to cinder,
Then up the chimney whirled,
And as it went, caught by the air
Each darkened cinder curled.

It frightened him, despite himself,
But still he held the club
Until the flames devoured it to
A withered little stub.

He washed himself and rubbed his clothes,
Blood was everywhere;
Even the paws of his fierce dog
Had thick blood on them there.

And every single moment
His eyes were turned onto
The cold corpse lying on the ground,
It chilled him through and through.

Now he was ready to depart
He backed towards the door,
And still his eyes were fixed upon
The body on the floor.

He dragged the dog behind him,
Then quietly as a mouse,
He softly closed the door – locked it –
And then he left the house.

He crossed the street and looking up,
Saw from down there – outside –
There was no sign of what the house
Now guiltily did hide.

There was the curtain, still pulled closed,
That Nancy would have drawn,
To let in light she'd never see –
For she'd not see the dawn.

For now she lay there where she fell –
He'd left her there to rot.
But dear God – how that bright sun
Poured down upon the spot.

He was so glad to quit the house,
His mind was in a fog.
He set off walking rapidly
And whistled to his dog.

He strode through Islington and then
Down to Highgate Hill,
Then carried on to Hampstead Heath,
And kept his pace up still.

He stumbled on throughout the day –
Bewildered, scared and fraught.
He wracked his brains on what to do
But all thoughts came to naught.

He headed on to Hatfield,
His every muscle strived
To put a distance from his crime,
And then when night arrived…

He found himself within a street,
A little bit run-down,
And there a stagecoach stood, it was
The mail from London town.

He sauntered up and heard a man
To another say,
'What's new down there in London then?
What's going on today?'

'Well nothing that I knows about,'
The other man replied.
'Corn's up a little in its price.'
The first man merely sighed.

'I heard about a murder though.
In Spitalfields, I think.
A dreadful murder, that it was.
Most likely caused by drink.'

'Was it a man or woman?'
'A woman,' said the man.
Sikes had cowered then and thought,
'I'll need to make a plan.'

He headed off and then for days
He wandered far and wide,
And all the time he saw her face –
Blank, staring and cold-eyed.

Sleeping rough just anywhere,
Alone and on the run,
And terrorised and haunted by
The dreadful deed he'd done.

Then after several desperate days,
His mood now very black,
He came to the decision that
'Twas best if he went back.

He thought, 'Down there in London is
The safest place to go,
The police will never think I'd choose
The city to lay low.

'I'll force old Fagin to supply
Some cash to get away.
Damn me – I'll go to France – I will –
And go without delay'

He whistled up his dog who had
Been chasing a young rabbit.
The animal approached him ,
Just out of force of habit.

But as Bill Sikes stooped down to tie
A 'kerchief round his throat,
The dog let out a deep, low growl,
Stepped back and shook its coat.

'Come back 'ere,' Sikes shouted out.
The dog, he wagged his tail.
Sikes called again, he thought that he
Would come and without fail.

This time the dog advanced, but then
Retreated – took no heed,
And then he paused then turned around
And scurried off at speed.

Sikes whistled out relentlessly.
He thought, 'He's acting weird.'
He waited there expectantly
But no dog reappeared.

Sikes shook his head in great dismay.
His mood turned very black,
For it was now quite clear – the dog
Would not be coming back.

MONKS AND MR BROWNLOW MEET

The twilight was now closing in
When Mr Brownlow stepped
From a hackney coach outside
The London house he kept.

Then two men thus alighted;
Rough, sturdy looking men.
Mr Brownlow gave a sign
And in a moment then…

They pulled a third from out the coach
And hurried him into
The house – and quickly then all four
Disappeared from view.

So what went on this evening?
Well these two burly hunks
Were there to handle the third man –
And *he* was evil Monks.

Once inside they went upstairs –
Monks with reluctant tread.
'If he hesitates or moves,'
Bold Mr Brownlow said…

'Why drag him down into the street
And then call up the police,
And say that he's a felon who
Has contravened the peace.'

'How dare you speak to me this way?'
Monks was filled with ire,
But Mr Brownlow stared right back
With eyes that were on fire.

'Why you are free to go,' he said.
'And of your own accord.
But if you go, I'll have you charged
With robbery and fraud.

'For I am quite immovable:
If you are too,' he said,
'Well then your blood be thus upon
Your own foul, evil head.'

'By whose authority?' cried Monks,
'Am I kidnapped today?
Brought here by those two mangy dogs
In this outrageous way.'

'By mine!' cried Mr Brownlow.
'I tell you and for sure,
If you dare think it best that you
Should seek help from the law…

'Why then 'twill be your fault alone
Just where that pathway ends,
For you'll be on your own – devoid
Of help or any friends.'

Monks muttered incoherently
And Mr Brownlow said,
'Make up your mind but be aware
The outcome's on your head.'

'Is there no compromise?' asked Monks.
Said Brownlow with a frown,
'Emphatically – no none at all.'
So Monks just sat right down.

He shrugged his shoulders – for he saw
Firm Brownlow's mind was set;
There was no way to thus escape
From his well cast, broad net.

'Lock the door,' Brownlow then told
His two attendants there.
'Come only if I ring,' he said,
Then sat down in a chair.

Monks asked, 'So now what's on your mind?
What is it you intend?
For this is pretty treatment from
My father's oldest friend.'

Mr Brownlow heaved a sigh.
He coughed then with a croak.
He cleared his throat quite noisily
And then he softly spoke.

'That is precisely why my boy
I act this way today,
And you had better listen now
To all I have to say.

'The wishes of my youthful years
Were bound to him for sure.
He very nearly once became
My chosen brother-in-law.

'His sister would have been my wife.
Oh what great love I felt,
But we were joined in grief as we
Beside her deathbed knelt.

'Because we suffered as we did,
Grief ridden, side by side,
We stayed close friends right up until
The dreadful day he died.

'These old associations
Are simply why – I vow
I'm lenient towards you and
I treat you gently now.

'Oh yes, young Edward Leeford,
I'm on to your sharp game,
And blush you may, but that fine sir
Is your true, proper name.'

'Well, this is all quite mighty fine,'
Monks said eventually.
'What's in a name, so tell me now
What do you want with me?'

'You have a brother,' Brownlow said.
'I saw the look of fear
When I approached you in the street
And whispered in your ear.

'I only spoke his name the once,
But from your look,' he said.
'I think I truly hit the nail
Most firmly on the head.'

'I have no brother,' Monks replied.
'I was an only child.
Your brash assertion is misplaced.
Quite off the beam and wild.'

But Mr Brownlow spoke out now.
He said, 'I've brought you here
To sort this business out for good;
To make the whole thing clear,

'And by the time we're good and done,
The awful sorry tale
Will be laid bare.' Monks sitting there
Now turned extremely pale.

So Mr Brownlow then began.
His voice, it rose and fell,
And Monks sat there and listened to
The tale he had to tell.

But inch by inch the truth came out,
And so to keep it short,
Here's an outline of the things
Good Brownlow did extort.

Yes it was true that Monks's name
Was as Brownlow said;
And Monks's dad was Brownlow's friend –
But now this friend was dead.

And ill-used Oliver and Monks
Truly were half-brothers.
They shared the selfsame father but
The pair had different mothers.

Monks's father hadn't loved
His wife, so sad to say
It was a cheerless marriage which
Was painful every day.

And then he fell in love and with
A charming, sweet young girl.
Agnes was her name and she
Just set his heart awhirl.

He said that he would marry her,
But then found out that he
Was left a great inheritance,
Abroad – in Italy.

It was a rich relation who
Had left a pile of cash,
So Monks's father set out then
In something of a dash…

To claim the money, bring it back –
But he stopped on the way,
To visit his friend Brownlow,
And leave with him that day…

A portrait of dear Agnes,
Which Brownlow hung with care.
It was the one that Oliver
Had seen when he'd been there.

The very one that had entranced
The eager little boy;
Which had for untold reason made
His sad heart leap with joy.

Whilst Monks's father was abroad
He had become unwell,
And gradually got worse and then,
We sadly here must tell…

He died and left young Agnes
In England all alone,
And she was pregnant now and faced
A future on her own.

He'd left a will behind him though,
And in it he proclaimed
Most of his money should be left
To his child, yet unnamed.

There was just one condition,
The child should live to be
A credit to his parents and
To all society.

He'd also there confessed that he
Was married and could not
Marry dear, sweet Agnes –
He couldn't tie the knot.

When Monks's mother heard of this
Her wailing was most shrill.
She found the documents and then
She burned the legal will.

She burned a letter he had left,
And so it came to be
She in a stroke destroyed proof of
The boy's identity.

Then Monks confessed that he had paid
Fagin to turn the boy
Into a thief – to make quite sure,
By this foul, devious ploy…

That Oliver would live a life
That surely ruled him out
Of ever making any claim –
And so without a doubt…

The money would be safe with Monks.
It would make certain sure,
There was no way that anyone
Could thus impose the law.

And finally – poor Agnes
Ran off – as well we know,
And died as she gave birth unto
Young Oliver and so…

This was how the details of
The sad boy's family,
Were now laid out for anyone
To very clearly see.

When all of this had been confessed
Stern Mr Brownlow said,
'Now will you sign a document
Admitting you've misled…

'And then make restitution –
Your brother must receive
The money he's entitled to
And then I do believe…

'Once this is done, why then you're free
To walk out through that door.
Go where you please for in this world
We need to meet no more.'

Monks was pacing up and down;
He wracked his brain to find
A way to just evade this course,
But no way came to mind.

While he was thinking desperately
The door was then unlocked,
And Dr Losberne entered.
He looked a little shocked.

He'd come to visit Brownlow
In quite a flurried state.
He'd come with information
To bring him up to date.

The pair were well acquainted.
For they'd been introduced
By Oliver and Rose for they
Had rightly both deduced…

The two reserved old gentlemen
Would get on well together,
For they were truly just like birds
Of the selfsame feather.

But Dr Losberne now spoke out,
His voice was very stern,
For he had something on his mind
As those there could discern.

'The man should now be taken;
They say, some time tonight.'
'The murderer?' asked Brownlow.
And Losberne said, 'That's right.

'His dog's been seen a-lurking
Around that Sikes's haunts,
Which likely means he's out about
On one of his vile jaunts.

'Beneath a cloak of darkness
Bill Sikes will be around;
Where the dog is – they believe –
This Sikes will too be found.

'Police are crawling everywhere
In every size and shape,
They've placed a hundred pounds reward –
The killer won't escape.'

'I'll give another fifty more,'
Old Brownlow did proclaim.
To see Sikes apprehended
Was now his heartfelt aim.

'And what of Fagin?' he then asked.
'Well, if I'm not mistaken,'
Said Dr Losberne – 'By this time
Old Fagin should be taken.

'The police were very confident
The villain would be found,
They're closing in and though the rogue
Has clearly gone to ground…

'The police think they'll soon have him;
In now but little time,
The devil will be made to pay
For his foul life of crime.'

Then Mr Brownlow turned to Monks,
'So will you do this task?
Will you agree to everything
And do just as I ask?'

Monks shifted then uneasily
And spoke in a low voice.
'I will,' he said – he realised
He had but little choice.

SIKES MEETS A GRISLY END

And now the police were closing in
For Sikes's whereabouts
Had been discovered and a throng,
With rough, ear-splitting shouts…

Had gathered round a building,
A scruffy, run-down place;
'Twas where Bill Sikes had chosen
To hide his evil face.

The word had travelled round the town,
Bill Sikes had now been found.
The police, they had him cornered in
The place he'd gone to ground.

They turned up in their hundreds
To see the killer's fall.
You should have heard them yell out loud,
Throw insults up and call.

Some people who were raging with
Self-justified, mad ire,
Suggested they should burn him out –
'Just set the house on fire.'

Another man came riding up
And jumped down from his horse.
'Bring a ladder,' he cried out.
'It is the only course.'

And so a mighty cry went up
And everyone got madder.
'Sledge-hammers – get some right away,
And someone bring a ladder.'

And high up in the building
The murderer looked down;
His face –a mask of anger – wore
The most horrendous frown.

The house was by the river
And Sikes thought he could see
How he might cheat the gathered throng,
And get away – be free.

'They're all afront the house,' he thought,
'So maybe I can hitch
A rope around something and drop
Into the Folly Ditch.

'It's on the other side of them.
I can avoid the fray.
I'll get a rope and drop right down
And clear off through that way.'

He grabbed a strong, long length of rope,
Then made his way up to
The roof of that old, creaking house
And then took in the view.

And there below were people.
He squinted through the black,
And realised their task had been
To guard the house's back.

The people yelled out noisily
To all those at the front,
And now they all came rushing round
To join the great manhunt.

Sikes looked across the parapet;
He saw the tide was out.
The ditch was just a bed of mud –
And then a mighty shout…

Rose up from down beneath him.
Triumphant walls of sound.
They echoed and re-echoed
Against the walls around.

It seemed the whole of London –
The city's population –
Had poured itself into the street
And with joined excitation…

Had come as one to curse him;
You should have heard the row.
And then one man cried out, 'Hurrah!
They've surely got him now.'

The angry crowd surged forward,
And then a mighty roar,
And then a cry went up to say,
At last, they'd forced the door.

And then the mob pushed harder,
And cries and shrieks were heard
For folk were being pressed and now
Great panic had occurred.

People struggled mindlessly
And in that moment then
Attention was diverted from
That evilest of men.

Sikes thought, 'This is my only chance.'
He thought this little glitch
Might give him just a moment
To drop into the ditch.

And then if he was lucky
His actions blessed conclusion,
Might be that he could creep off in
The darkness and confusion.

Roused now to strength and energy,
From noise within the house,
And with the fire of panic which
No strength of will could douse…

He grabbed the stack of chimneys,
And tightly tied the rope
Around them and with silent prayers –
And with a deal of hope…

He made a strong and running noose
Around the other end,
And using it with utmost care
He hoped then to descend.

But at the very moment
He took the rope in hand,
And brought the loop across his head,
Intent to then expand…

The loop to go beneath his arms –
Well at that moment he
Looked behind him on the roof
To see what he could see.

He threw his arms above his head
And with a yell of terror
He cried, 'It's Nancy's eyes again!'
It was a fatal error;

For now he staggered backwards
As if then struck by lightning.
He lost his balance – tumbled –
The whole scene very frightening.

The noose was at his throat – it ran
And closed around his neck.
There was no way to stop it.
It ran without a check.

He fell for five-and-thirty feet;
The crowd all went berserk.
They shouted out in horror – then
There was a sudden jerk.

A terrible convulsion
As his limbs were flung
Out in all directions, then –
He silently just hung.

The chimney quivered with the shock
But it withstood the fall,
And there the lifeless body swung
Against the wooden wall.

A dog that had lain quite concealed,
Appeared now on the roof.
It ran around and then let out
A sad and plaintiff woof.

A dismal howl resounded then,
The likes of which to wring
Great sympathy from any heart,
Then with a lithesome spring…

He jumped towards his master there –
Bill Sikes – he of that name.
He leapt towards his shoulders but
Was careless in his aim.

He fell into the ditch and hit
His head upon a stone.
He lay there dead – above him swung
The only friend he'd known.

FAGIN'S LAST NIGHT ALIVE

Fagin was apprehended
And he was put on trial,
And though the evil reprobate
Was in complete denial…

He was condemned as guilty.
The judge put on his cap
And sentenced Fagin then to death.
Old Fagin seemed to snap…

For he just stared about him –
His muttering began.
He mumbled softly to himself,
'I'm just a poor, old man.'

And then they led him from the court
And placed him on his own,
In a cell wherein he sat
Upon a bench of stone.

The cell was cold and miserable;
The walls were damp and grey,
And Fagin sat – immovable,
Throughout that dismal day.

And then it grew to be quite dark,
And as he sat alone,
He began to think about
The many men he'd known…

Who'd died upon the scaffold –
He'd watched some of them die.
He'd joked for some of them had prayed.
He'd even seen some cry.

Then the night came on – it was
Dark, dismal, silent, bare.
Scared Fagin heard the church clock strike.
It caused him quite a scare.

To people who are free, the sound
Speaks of the coming day.
It heralds life and looks towards
The sun's soft, warming ray.

But to old Fagin cowering there
The iron bell's great boom
Came laden as a hollow sound
Steeped in a massive gloom.

For as he shook and beat his breast
And took each tortured breath,
The awful sound spoke out to him
Of just one thing – 'twas Death.

And as the morning came he knew
This was his last full day.
Another night – and then the end –
And then men came to pray.

They knelt there with doomed Fagin,
Chanting out their verses,
He drove the well intentioned men
Away – and with loud curses.

And so the night fell once again.
His last night in the world.
And now a desperate, helpless mood
Across him thus unfurled.

All hope of mercy had long gone.
His conscience tortured so.
Never had a prisoner
Been driven down so low.

He cowered on his hard, stone bed.
This night would be his last.
He thought about the things he'd done,
His evil, wretched past.

His bloodless face was white as snow.
His beard was torn and twisted,
And still the awful, dreadful thoughts
Were with him and persisted.

His eyes shone with an awful light.
A fever burnt his frame.
His unwashed flesh, it crackled –
And time ticked on the same.

And then the clocks chimed midnight.
He was in such a state.
He dreaded when the dawn would come,
For he would die at eight.

And then he heard the jailor speak.
He called his name to see
If Fagin was awake – He cried,
'Why Fagin – yes that's me.'

'There's someone wants to see you.'
Fagin shook his head.
'What right have they to butcher me?
Why, strike them all down dead!'

Then as he spoke he spotted them.
Mr Brownlow and
He stood there holding Oliver
By the young lad's hand.

Oliver had asked to see
The wretch before he died,
And so he walked towards the man,
To stand there by his side.

'Let me say a prayer,' he said.
'Just kneel upon one knee,
And say one prayer, I beg of you.
Please kneel down here with me.'

But Fagin cried, 'Outside! Outside!'
His voice was now a shout.
'You can save me – they'd trust you,
For you can get me out.'

'Oh God forgive the wretched man,'
Cried Oliver in shock,
But now they turned away – they heard
The jailor turn the lock.

They left old Fagin crying out.
They left him there behind,
And as they went they were convinced
That he had lost his mind.

The moon was shining as they left
And there out in the yard,
They saw the awful blackened stage,
With a man on guard.

A bare cross-beam – a rope hung down.
Oliver caught his breath;
For there they saw the hideous
Apparatus – of Death!

AT LAST

And so our tale draws to a close,
But it remains to say
That Oliver met his brother Monks
On one eventful day.

Mr Brownlow set it up
And Monks confessed it all.
It was such information with
The power to appal.

For Oliver was overcome
To hear his brother say
That Fagin and his gang of thieves
Had all been in his pay.

Then Mr Brownlow told the boy
The strangest thing of all;
It really was extraordinary
That it should thus befall.

For Rose – his own sweet, darling Rose.
Yes Rose – and no-one other,
Was the younger sister of
Oliver's poor mother.

Yes Agnes was her sister.
Oh what a thing to be.
It surely was the strangest thing
For all of them to see.

So Oliver hugged his loving aunt
And knew they'd always stay
Close to each other evermore,
For every coming day.

In time Rose Maylie married
A fine, upstanding man,
And Mrs Maylie lived with them;
They formed a happy clan.

Then on investigation
It turned out to be
The money that Monks had in hand
Was not that much, you see.

So Mr Brownlow made the case
To split the sum in two.
He had no wish to ruin Monks –
'Twas proper thing to do.

And Oliver most joyfully
Agreed to this sound plan,
The hope was that in time bad Monks
Would be a decent man.

And Monks, still bearing that same name,
Once this had been unfurled
Took the cash and left these shores
And sailed to the New World.

We sadly here must now relate
He squandered, once abroad,
The money and then quickly turned
To knavery and fraud.

He sank right to the bottom
And left behind a trail
Of grave dishonesty and so
Then found himself in jail.

Through everything he'd cheated,
He'd robbed and conned and lied.
Then finally in prison
The bad, sad man had died.

Mr Brownlow, once all things
Were sorted and well done,
Took steps to make young Oliver
His dearest, legal son.

For he adopted him and then
With Mrs Bedwin too
Moved to the place where Rose now lived,
And so it's surely true…

This happy little group – these folk –
Had all as one unfurled
A scene of happiness as great
As known in this old world.

And Dr Losberne then became
Close friends with Grimwig, so
The pair enjoyed companionship
As good as one could know.

And what of Fagin's gang? – Well they
Were split up by the law,
And Dodger did some time in jail,
And we all hope for sure…

That in time he'll change his ways.
We hope this will be true,
But with a chap like Dodger, there's
No telling what he'll do.

And Charley Bates, well here's a thing –
Took very little time
To change his ways because he'd been
Appalled by Sikes's crime.

He became a farmer's drudge
And struggled much at first.
Sometimes he worked so hard he thought
His lungs would surely burst.

But in time the lad got on,
And now we're pleased to tell,
The last time he was heard of
He was doing rather well.

And what of Mr Bumble?
And his most devious wife.
Well things have all gone wrong and they
Now live a life of strife.

For in time the pair became –
Although still fat and large –
Paupers in the Workhouse where
They both were once in charge.

And finally we here must tell
That in the small church where
Young Oliver now prayed there was
A marble tablet there.

And written on the tablet
Was just a single word,
As fine a word as ever known
Or really ever heard.

That single word was 'Agnes'.
There was no flowery wreath.
And sad to say no coffin
Lay there underneath.

But if the spirits of the dead
Return from up above
To a place where they will find
A true, abiding love…

Well, Agnes must return – and then
Find some peace of mind,
Knowing that the little boy
She had to leave behind…

Is safe now with her sister,
And Mr Brownlow – so
This really is a comforting
And joyful thing to know.

Also by Richard Cuddington

SHAKESPEARE'S TRAGEDIES
IN EASY READING VERSE

Richard Cuddington applies his Easy Reading Verse to Shakespeare's Tragedies. These are some of the Bard's most famous and compelling plays. Retold here in simple and engaging verse, the drama and excitement unfold with an urgency and momentum that captures the essence of the original plays.

Here the reader will meet Hamlet avenging his father's murder, Romeo risking all for his Juliet, Othello borne down with jealousy, Macbeth plotting to obtain Scotland's crown and many other colourful and doomed characters.

The sheer drama of some of Shakespeare's most memorable and highly acclaimed plays is captured here in fast moving, entertaining verse.

And when you know what each play is about you may well be encouraged to find out more about what makes these people tick by venturing into the original texts, having crept under the literary barrier and already found a way in by the back door.

SHAKESPEARE'S COMEDIES IN EASY READING VERSE

Richard Cuddington offers his readers a new approach to Shakespeare which acknowledges the Bard's stature as England's finest poet and playwright but lays aside the trappings of that greatness to reveal what made him popular with his contemporary audiences and what can still enchant us today – the stories.

Here in Easy Reading Verse the author retells the stories of Shakespeare's Comedies with clarity, humour and a modern directness. Readers will meet Shylock demanding his pound of flesh, Jack Falstaff pursuing his 'merry wives', Petruchio taming his Katherine and many other unforgettable characters who leap off the page with the immediacy of cartoon personalities.

The straightforward language with its bouncing, infectious rhythms and uncomplicated verse add pace and humour to each story as it rapidly unfolds. In this way the author makes Shakespeare less intimidating to potential readers, showing that England's greatest playwright can be fun and encouraging all who enjoy these verses to sample the rich pleasure of the original work.

SHAKESPEARE'S HISTORIES & ROMANCES IN EASY READING VERSE

Here in Richard Cuddington's Easy Reading Verse are
Shakespeare's Histories and Romances which take the
reader on two separate journeys. One through various
turbulent periods of English history – the other through
the slightly calmer waters of romance.
All the stories are told in clear and rhythmic verse which
enhances the many dramatic and romantic situations.
Readers will be entranced by the very diversity and
richness of the colourful plots.
Here we meet Richard the Second losing his throne,
Henry the Fifth conquering the French at Agincourt and
Richard the Third using all his dastardly wiles to keep the
crown. In contrast the Romances will introduce Prospero
whipping up a tempest, Pericles losing, then finding his
Thaisa and Palamon and Arcite fighting for the hand of
Emilia. A veritable pageant of drama, turmoil and intrigue
is encapsulated in these enthralling stories which are truly
some of the Bard's finest plays.
These adaptations are an enjoyable and riveting read and
act as an excellent bridge to the original texts.

SHAKESPEARE'S SONNETS
IN EASY READING VERSE

Richard Cuddington's light-hearted adaptation of
Shakespeare's Sonnets captures the essence of the original
texts but in a way that makes them instantly accessible and
understandable to the modern reader.

Originally published in 1609, many critics believe the
Sonnets come closer to revealing Shakespeare the man,
than any of his other works. Written in the first person,
the Sonnets expose an emotional range that has given
them enduring appeal.

The author now applies his straightforward Easy Reading
Verse to create a fresh interpretation of the Sonnets. Here
in simple and enjoyable lyrics, the mysteries of the
Sonnets are unravelled, and with the original texts also
contained within the book, they act as an aid in the
understanding of Shakespeare's masterpieces.

CHAUCER'S CANTERBURY TALES IN EASY READING VERSE

For all its great reputation and the affection in which it is held, Chaucer's Canterbury Tales, written in 14th century Middle English, can actually be a daunting prospect to read. Richard Cuddington now steps in with a novel approach to Chaucer's famous gallery of pilgrims with their tales of chivalry, romance, courtly love, treachery, avarice, bawdiness, humour and nobility.

Whether you're new to the tales, or perhaps a teacher looking to enthuse and stimulate your students, or simply thinking of re-reading them, you will find here a thoroughly entertaining and immediately accessible way in to the storytelling genius of Chaucer in simple and amusing rhyming verse.

CHARLES DICKENS' A CHRISTMAS CAROL IN EASY READING VERSE

Charles Dickens' A Christmas Carol is arguably the most dearly loved Christmas story ever written – a favourite with the whole family. Whether you are one of the many fans of the story or possibly even new to the tale – you will surely enjoy this adaptation, written in fast moving, light-hearted verse. Author Richard Cuddington, who has already adapted the complete works of Shakespeare and Chaucer's Canterbury Tales into fun filled, narrative verse, now applies his rhythmic style to this famous classic. Here is Scrooge in all his miserly misery, slowly being converted from his former monstrous self into a being who really knows how to celebrate Christmas. The charming verse takes us on an unstoppable journey where we meet the Spirits of Christmas Past, Present and Future, the joyful Mr Fezziwig and of course, the tragic but lovable figure of Tiny Tim. And on the way Scrooge dominates a tale that celebrates the joy of Christmas, encouraging a belief that we should embrace its spirit throughout the year.

**KENNETH GRAHAME'S
THE WIND IN THE WILLOWS
IN EASY READING VERSE**

Here is a delightful re-telling of one of Britain's best-loved books, aimed at younger children but also providing a treat for Grahame's established legion of fans of all ages. Richard Cuddington's verse rendition of Kenneth Grahame's The Wind in the Willows is the perfect introduction to a volume of stories which have enchanted generations of readers with its timeless evocation of life 'along the river bank'. All the well-known characters are here: the Mole, the Water Rat, Badger, Otter and, of course, the larger-than-life and utterly irrepressible Mr Toad of Toad Hall. The author has retained all the verve and energy of the original tales, but simplified the language to make them more accessible to the younger reader. Mole's frightening visit to the Wild Wood in the depths of winter and the colourful adventures of Toad take centre stage in bubbling rhythmic verse that drives the ebullient narrative forward so that there is never a dull moment.

9 781849 149570